The Plasma

To Ramesh, Senthil, Param
& Barbara
BRENDA,

[signature]
12.08.2019

The Plasma

Kamalendu Malaker

© 2018 Kamalendu Malaker
All rights reserved.

ISBN-13: 9781981743957
ISBN-10: 1981743952
Library of Congress Control Number: 2017919407
CreateSpace Independent Publishing Platform
North Charleston, South Carolina

To my late parents—my father, Dr. Manasa Charan Malaker, and my mother, Shoroshi Malaker.
And to my patients and students—from whom I have learned more than I have given them.

CONTENTS

Acknowledgments · ix

Chapter 1	Life Is Great· ·	1
Chapter 2	Dreamland America· · · · · · · · · · · · · · · · · · · ·	5
Chapter 3	Job! What Job?· ·	11
Chapter 4	Found My Love ·	19
Chapter 5	Beginning of a Honeymoon · · · · · · · · · · · · ·	27
Chapter 6	Hectic Life ·	31
Chapter 7	The Flu Season ·	36
Chapter 8	My First Visit to a Specialist · · · · · · · · · · · · ·	40
Chapter 9	My Next Visits to the Specialists· · · · · · · · · ·	44
Chapter 10	My Fourth Visit to the Specialist · · · · · · · · ·	50
Chapter 11	Phone Call ·	55
Chapter 12	The Journey Begins ·	64
Chapter 13	Tests and Investigations Begin · · · · · · · · · · ·	70
Chapter 14	Return to Boston: Relief with Joy · · · · · · · · ·	77
Chapter 15	Our First Trip to Tijuana · · · · · · · · · · · · · · ·	86
Chapter 16	My Second Day in the Tijuana Hospital· · · · · · · ·	89
Chapter 17	My Third Visit to Tijuana · · · · · · · · · · · · · · ·	95
Chapter 18	My Strange Visitors in Tijuana · · · · · · · · · · ·	98
Chapter 19	The Next Three Years · · · · · · · · · · · · · · · · · ·	102
Chapter 20	Mary-Ann the Savior· · · · · · · · · · · · · · · · · · ·	107
Chapter 21	Mary-Ann Saves Me Again · · · · · · · · · · · · · ·	113
Chapter 22	My Wife and Children Drift Away · · · · · · · · ·	119
Chapter 23	Dream Come True: Visiting My People · · · · · · · ·	124

Chapter 24	The Last Voyage	133
Chapter 25	The Emissary Appears	140
Chapter 26	Mary-Ann's Confession	146
	About the Author	157

ACKNOWLEDGMENTS

It is just not an acknowledgment but a confession that without the unending patience and support from my beloved wife, Baljit; my darling daughter, Sharmeela; our princess granddaughter, Anaya; and my son-in-law, Jagdeep, it would have been impossible to do something that I normally would not have done. I did it with passion and compassion for them all.

I come from a large family. All my brothers are successful and well respected in their own right, in their professions of choice. We are scattered all over the world, and to us distance has very little meaning. As a family, we stayed close and became inspired by one another's success and failures. We took our mutual love, respect, and well-wishes for granted and never really appreciated the profound impact we all had on one another. My eldest brother is Amal, and younger brother, Nirmal, is a banker turned apothecary and spiritual guide. The untimely death of Shyamal, an industrialist, deeply impacted the dynamics of our family. Sajal (Buro) gained fame as a highly respected surgeon and a connoisseur of art and culture in the state of Orissa, India, and Utpal (Bachhu) was highly successful in his engineering career and is now enjoying several intellectual pursuits after retirement. The youngest, Parimal, a marine engineer of international repute, is an active contributor to the progress of art and culture, which has made him a regional and national celebrity.

Our two sisters played the role of mother, especially the second sister, Kalyanee Charkraborty (Kinu). She is the brightest among us and kept the entire family culturally and intellectually thriving with her multiple talents. I can't help but remember my late cousin Bimal Malaker (same age as me), who got me into writing. While I was his mentor for his literary activities, they inadvertently became mine. I feel I have to fulfill his dreams that were unmet.

Lastly but most importantly, outside the family, I would like to acknowledge Dr. Norman Coleman at the Harvard Joint Center for Radiation Oncology with his ever-forgiving personality, kindness, enthusiasm for life and living, intellectualism, and appreciation for free-thinking, out-of-this-world ideas (of course, that is Harvard). His inspiration—be it academic, research, or my wild adventures in untrodden parts of the globe—all has had a lasting impact on everything I did after I left Harvard.

I also acknowledge the untiring effort of my secretary, Amina Toussaint, for not only retyping the manuscript but also spending hours editing the content to its presentable shape.

CHAPTER 1

LIFE IS GREAT

It seemed like only yesterday that I left this place. This was the place where I was born fifty-four years ago. Nothing much had changed. The house—the room where I was born—was still there. The porch where I grew up, the river by the side of the house, the dense tropical forest covering mountains on the back, the narrow paths leading to the riverbank, and the coarse and rugged hilly lanes going up the hill could all still be seen, except now they looked sad for lack of a human touch. There were several houses along the riverbank, on the high slope of the mountain. Those houses were still there, yet no children jumped over the fences. The chickens were quiet. The goats, yes! The goats sat idle, as if they had forgotten to munch on grass, yet there was plenty around. In fact the grassy patches that my family and neighbors had cleared for farming and for our goats, cows, pigs, and chickens to roam around seemed to have no roamers. Yet the fresh sea breeze and the smell of cinnamon trees and other tropical fruits spreading their essence from up the mountain down to the foothills passing our village made us believe in the blissful heaven, full of milk and honey.

As I walked up the stream along the village road, I passed house after house, cottages, and shacks where few, very few, seemed awake. It was sleepy, very sleepy. Occasionally someone from the veranda, in a faint but very welcoming voice, said, "Good day, sir. Take care; the path is rugged. Watch for the falling rocks from the hills." It had rained a lot, and rainwater carried stones, rocks, and boulders of all sizes and shapes. Often they were stuck on their way down and decided to roll down other times, when no one was expecting a shower of boulders.

I could barely see the man sitting in an armchair on the porch of his house, not far from the rugged lane I was trying to walk up. I thought to myself the old man would not mind if I went back, returned his courtesy, and introduced myself.

He was in his eighties, aging but not old. He spoke clearly, deliberately, yet in a very soft, kind, welcoming voice.

"I am James, your neighbor," I said.

He knew my great-uncle and his family, who lived in our house, but not me.

"Oh! You must like any land but your home. See! So many houses along the river—most of us, like you, did leave but returned to where we were born and grew up. The soil, the air, the trees, forest, river, and the sea—those gave us the courage to leave and strength to return," he said without stopping or mincing his words. Then he said, "Are you back? Thinking of coming back? Or just passing by?"

He had so much intimacy in his voice that I forgot that I had just come to see if my folks were still around, if the house was standing or had been washed away by torrential rain or blown to pieces by tropical storms.

The man said, "Your fear is real; be bold and gather yourself together to return and see the place of your birth, your growth, your dreams that I presume have come true. Like me, I am sure you will like to return to this place."

A voice from my inside said, *Yes, I want to, forever, where I will not be ever sold as a slave in any form, shape, or kind.*

I must have spoken aloud. I was also surprised—what a stupid thought. What slave? Where? When? How? It must be thoughts from my ancestors reeling in my mind as I backtracked myself. I had such a wonderful life in Boston, a haven of opportunity, opulence, luxury, and grace. No fear of being a slave.

I looked around but did not see the house or the gentleman. Then I realized that I had walked away from him without saying good-bye. I went back. The house was locked, dark, with no sign of the armchair or the beautiful porch.

I thought, *Maybe I am at the wrong house. I will come back tomorrow to catch up with him.* I strolled back to my childhood home. It was dark by then, but the village was very bright. The roads had electricity; every house had a bright electric bulb at the entrance. Very different from when I had left thirty-five years ago.

Tomorrow came. I took a walk in the opposite direction until I reached the foothill and the main road—the walk I had taken every day for nearly twelve years to take the bus to my school. The road was there; the bus stand was there. Now there was a weather shelter to protect waiting bus riders from the elements of nature. Scorching sun, blowing wind, torrential tropical rain, blowing tree parts—I had withstood all those for twelve memorable years without the protection of a shelter. Memories came in abundance, but events were few, so few that I could see and count them on one hand. Some left deep scars in my mind; others were overflowing fountains of happiness, even today.

I walked toward my old school. It was not there. Instead a big gas station stood there. The people inside told me that the school had moved up the hill onto its new premises. I could see the new school at a distance. That did not bring out any old memories, but the gas station did. I stood by the gas station—for how long I do not know—until the horn of a bus woke me up to get off its lane.

I did not care if the school walked away from me, but the land on which it stood once, the playground, the slow stream—they stoked my memories, my real memories of my childhood in that school for twelve years. The years I was away, I never missed my old school. But coming back after thirty-five years, my mind was full of the thrill and excitement of a schoolboy who did not do much but loved watching others doing things. These visions brought back a flurry of memories, but none of them matched the dream of being back at home with my family and friends.

Fountain of happiness indeed, but none better than a dream.

The dream was gone, and the pain was back. I was wide awake in a hospital bed, somewhere on the West Coast of the United States of America. California, maybe, maybe not, but a hospital bed no doubt. Drip stands with monitors bleeped and kicked away, a stark reminder of where I was.

"James! It is no fun, and it is certainly not funny," a voice said.

It was Mary-Ann, who was sitting by my bed. Mary-Ann was my partner now. My partner in all respects—indeed, partner to the hilt.

"How do you feel, James? Did you sleep well? I could hear you murmuring for the last two hours. You have been talking about your village, your father, your mother, your neighbors, your school, a bus, something about a gas station. You were very clear, as if you were telling me the story of your childhood."

I was stunned. A dream, but it was so real that I felt like I was back in my days in my village as a schoolboy.

Mary-Ann said, "It could be the effect of the medication they gave to sedate you for the procedure."

"Procedure? What procedure?" I said. "I did not know I had to have a procedure."

"Do not worry, my dear," said Mary-Ann. "Wake up. I will help you to wash up, and breakfast will be here soon. You need not go to the lounge. They give you wonderful breakfasts here. I love the food, in or out of the hospital. Don't you think so, James?" asked Mary-Ann. "Here comes the breakfast lady. Oh, it is for two of us. Good, I do not have to leave you alone."

"Do not worry, Mary-Ann! I am fine, fit, and ferocious."

"You are something else, James. Now let us take care of the breakfast."

CHAPTER 2

DREAMLAND AMERICA

After I finished my high school, I was wondering what to do next. My family expected me to help them on their farm. But I was not ready for it. I saw planes flying over our house; I saw huge ships, multiple stories high, looking like big hotels you see in movies, except they floated on ocean water, carrying thousands of people from faraway lands to our shores for a day or a few hours and then floating away and disappearing into the horizon, just as the planes fly into the faraway sky not to be seen again. I knew I couldn't be in any of those, but my desire to go to other people's shores got stronger after the passing of each ship or flying plane.

In school, we learned about oceans, rivers, countries, nations, war, disasters, kings, queens, dictators, savages, man-eaters, deserts, thousands-of-miles-long rivers with alligators and anacondas, and tribes living in tents and those in igloos, but never did we learn about what was there just beyond our shores, where the planes were flying to or the huge palace boats were sailing to.

I was born and raised in my little island home, which one could walk from top to bottom in two days and side to side in just over a day—if one walked briskly and if there had been no mountains or 365 rivers raging or streaming from the high land to the sea. The rivers' journey was hardly ever more than twenty miles from the peaks of the mountains to their submission at sea.

Watching TV and cinemas and looking at colorful magazines, I saw huge expanses of land, miles and miles of grassland, dense forests, snow-peaked mountains, cities full of people, crowds and crowds, cars and cars, buildings dozens and dozens of stories high, and wide never-ending roads. The places they could take me were unimaginable; consciously, subconsciously, or even unconsciously, it was beyond my imagination how those faraway lands might look in reality.

Such a land was America, I heard from my parents, neighbors, siblings, teachers, friends, and any other codreamers. I heard it most loudly from my uncle who lived in Boston for many years.

After completing his schooling, my uncle helped his dad fish in small boats from sunrise to sunset in the Caribbean waters. He learned the fishing trade from his dad and landed in Boston. He was a smart, well-spoken, and impressive character, a practical dreamer who possessed a well-crafted physique and tireless stamina and energy.

He gathered a few black men around, looking to discover them in foreign lands, which were to some extent hostile in every respect. He bought a small fishing boat, more like a dinghy, and started his fishing trips to Atlantic coasts from Boston. That was almost forty years ago. Now he owned several fishing trawlers, and several black, white, and brown men work for him; that was what my mom told me. He was a real inspiration to me. As a toddler, I remember him as a big bully, daring, but a very kind person who was always there for anyone from the community who needed his help. Although he was actually my mother's cousin, I grew up calling him my uncle since my mom always considered him to be her brother. My mom told me he was my uncle, so I got the courage to write to him in spite of his being a big black man in America. Before the week was up, a telephone call came from Boston. I was stunned and more than surprised to hear an elderly voice, which my mom told me was my uncle from Boston.

With no preamble, he said, "Young man, you want to come to America—you got it. Get ready, pack your bag, and pick up your airline ticket at the airport. I will pick you up at the Boston airport.

We will talk about a job when we meet; make sure your passport and any other documents you need to travel are in order and up to date."

Click! The telephone was disconnected.

Apparently it was my mom who was the main actor in this drama. She later told me that she had been corresponding with her cousin for the last several months and was able to convince him it would be a sure "investment" and that he would never look back.

Indeed, he never had to as long as he was around. I was not stupid but gentle and soft-spoken, and I generally kept my calm and composure in a crisis. My uncle liked my personality and was a mentor from the time I arrived in Boston until he passed away seven years ago.

His business office was outside Boston, although he had lived in Roxbury ever since he had landed in America.

His house was bigger than any in my country. It was very big with gadgets of all forms, all sizes, all serving a different purpose. His garage could easily hold three big cars.

The high concentration of African Americans in the Roxbury area was its main attraction for him. There he found his welcoming neighbors, educated and cultured blacks, and he was close to many highly reputed academic, research, and health-care centers. Unfortunately, during his lifetime, the neighborhood experienced a gradual deterioration of social standards, safety, and general lifestyle. Still, I could not believe that a black man in America could have so much wealth.

For me, Roxbury was like a homecoming, with a twist. It was not my Caribbean island home. It has tall houses, noisy cars, big wide clean roads, and people busy running for something or some place to go. It had marked roads and traffic lights, and it was very orderly and very different from the big cities I had seen in the Caribbean.

I was told that Boston was not exactly what American cities were like. It was much quieter and teeming with young people rushing with a sparkle in their eye. Other big American cities were different.

New York, Chicago, Los Angeles, San Francisco, Atlanta, Washington, Houston, Oklahoma, Phoenix, San Diego, Fargo-Moorhead, and many more were all American; they all had many things in common. But Boston was different.

To me, Boston was different. This was where I first discovered myself. This was where I found the woman I love the most—my wife, Marina. This was where my three lovely and beautiful daughters were born. This was where I became an adult, a grown-up and responsible member of the community. No one questioned my color, my faith, and even my gender. This was where I worked and built up my reputation as a reliable, fair, and an honest businessman. I started as a fishing boat's mate, then bookkeeper of a fish-export company, then an animal caretaker of a famous research laboratory, and then at last a business owner breeding small animals for several famous Boston academic and research institutes.

The transformation from a fisherman's mate to a businessman shows that in America everything is possible, no matter if you are white, brown, yellow, or black. Yet I can't pause and forget my uncle, his affection, his mentorship, his hawkish attention, and his unlimited energy and enthusiasm that set my American life toward achieving my American dream.

As I settled in my uncle's home in Boston, I was just getting used to his lavish way of life. I had no idea that a black man could own a house like this, even keeping a housemaid to look after the house, and drive Mercedes cars. In my mind, a black man driving an expensive car must be with the mafia or might be himself a part of the mafia in his own right. The picture we get from the TV shows and Hollywood films couldn't be farther from the truth.

One day my uncle told me, "James! We are going fishing for a few days, and you are coming with me."

"Of course," I said.

A large fishing boat, the likes of which I had never seen in the waters of our shores back in the Caribbean, was in front of me. He said it was a deepwater fishing boat; we would get back home in three or four days. I was excited about the experience I was about to get.

To my distress and disappointment, as soon as the boat started rolling, my stomach started churning; I felt sick and vomited all over, and my shipmates had to take care of me. For three days and three nights, I was in bed with virtually no food and very little drink. We returned to Boston on the fourth day, a huge loss for my uncle's fishing expedition.

A couple of weeks later, he asked me again to come with him for another fishing trip. This time we were prepared for the worst seasickness that could occur on a boat at sea. I was determined that I would never let it happen again. But to my dismay, as soon as the boat started, even before it started to sail, I felt violently sick, even after all the medications I had taken on doctor's orders to prevent seasickness. It seemed to be all in vain!

So I said to my uncle, "Fishing is not my way of life. I must look beyond."

I started to work in his office as a bookkeeper. I was poor in math, very careless with my figures; I had no experience in bookkeeping, nor do I have any longing for it.

He realized that in spite of me trying hard to do my best, my best was worse than his expectations. He told me to take a break, wander around the city, or for that matter, go around the country on my own and meet people in different jobs, professions, or even the jobless and homeless and learn from them in regard to how they coped. There are lots of black people who are homeless and jobless in America. Yet they would not leave the country for opportunities elsewhere. Such is the lure of the American dream, where one can jump from rags to riches if one has the right thinking, perseverance, and attitude.

So I plodded along from city to city, from motels to motels, jumping from buses to trains and back again. I just walked the streets aimlessly all day. Yet later I realized how aimless one was walking the streets, lanes, and byways; one really need not have an aim. It is the aim that aims at you. The aim is to aim at passersby who are aiming at you.

After scouting the country, scouring various neighborhoods, seeing the magnificent sights of the country, and making some friends and alienating others, I returned to Boston.

Yet I had no idea what was best for me. How could I make a living? I had finished my high-school education with good grades. I should not be living off my uncle. I was no help to his business either. A sense of guilt and desperation was setting in my mind although there was no need.

Knowing my uncle, I knew that he would tell me to continue to explore possibilities until I found the one that suited me and was to my liking. But he rejected any idea of going back to school. He kept saying, "Your learning at school is to forget whatever you learn in classes, but your learning at work is forever."

CHAPTER 3

JOB! WHAT JOB?

I had to do something. I had to be useful. I turned twenty, and in my village back in the Caribbean, I would be expected to be a mature adult. My uncle gave me ideas, introduced me to people of various jobs and businesses, and was never angry or upset but always encouraging.

"I have been through it all," said he. "Wait for the proper opportunity." What he discouraged me to be was a "burger flipper."

I had been in Boston for more than six months, and I wanted to offer some financial help to my aging parents, who were also looking after my three younger sisters and two brothers. They were all at school. My parents were farmers of crops and dairy. They lived a comfortable life. After all expenses, they still managed to save a little, which they had spent to send me to Boston. Now it was time to pay them back.

Boston was teeming with young people: university folks, college students, high-school boys—not only American whites but also people from all over the world, all colors, and men and women. There were big tower blocks, companies, cargo-filled ships in the jetties, shops full of people in fancy clothing, students with their backpacks. There was an air of business, seriousness, and maturity; even with so many young people around, nobody was hurrying. There was no pushing, no elbowing, no screaming, and no road rage.

With so many activities and so much happening, I should have been able to find something that would set me up for a career. At any point in time, the city hosted a quarter of a million students and around thirty-five universities. Longwood Avenue, which cut through Harvard Medical School, major hospitals, and research centers, also housed a variety of restaurants and takeout places, cafés, and cafeterias. At Harvard Square, the greatness was even more thriving, and choices were numerous.

Back in Roxbury in one of my pensive moments, I was sitting in one of our neighboring Starbucks on a dull, cold, snowy day, when the roads were slushy and cars on it were painfully sluggish. One car got stuck in the slush; to get out of its deathtrap, it was going back and forth. As it was trying to maneuver itself out of the slush, it was sinking more and more and spreading mud and slush 360 degrees like confetti.

Covered up with thick winter garments, another black man entered the Starbucks. It was very cold out there. The Boston cold was piercing; it cut through your flesh and chewed the bones. Thick wool was not always enough protection. He started to peel himself out of his layers of cold-fighting armor. When it was all done, he was not a black man at all, not even a brown man, but a white man with a blondish head full of hair, in his midfifties, just short of six feet, who physically appeared like a nightclub bouncer.

He ordered his "black double-double mocha" and gently took the table next to mine. He was carrying a book, anticipating a long break from fighting the cold, slush, and splashes from the passing cars.

I was feeling sorry for him and greeted him.

"Good day, sir," I said. "Thanks to Starbucks for giving shelter to so many cold-struck Bostonians. All over the world, in cold or heat, Starbucks is always there to comfort you, no matter what state of mind or body you are in."

He stared at me for seconds and said, "Hi d'ere."

Aha! This was not a Bostonian or even standard American greeting—or maybe it was American. How much did I know about this country anyway?

"Back at home," said he, "we hardly talk about weather, snow, heat, sweat, hurricanes, tornadoes, or for that matter, any kind of storm. It is so sunny year round that sometimes we need to imagine the bad weather and live through our imagination. The weather is so boringly beautiful and sunny that one has to get out of the enchantment."

The more he spoke, the more I felt that he was a white non-American.

Maybe I needed to understand more about this man, get to know him better. Maybe he had some common woes and goals with me. Maybe he was a foreigner and trying to catch his American dream, like me. Maybe he also came from a small Caribbean island, where islands are our world—we are born there, grow up there, go to school, get jobs, get married, have families, grow old, and retire. People come from vast continents to the islands to retire, but where can the islanders go to retire? Nowhere—they die there, believing that is the beginning and end of the universe and humanity.

Somehow, I had always been fascinated about knowing others, not necessarily those who looked like us, spoke like us, or dressed or ate like us. In the towns and villages, one saw very little of anyone not like us; we were content in our universe, surrounded by the vast ocean. Although we all knew that we did come to the islands from vast lands beyond the oceans, far away from our shores, the islands were our universe, and their people were the limits of the boundary of our humanity and that of civilization. We were happy as we were; those from outside from the island were aliens. We were not interested in aliens. But I was indeed just the opposite. I liked to know people, those who were not like us and not from the island.

In no time, we started to converse, partly as a distraction from the cold, which we had both waded through not so long ago.

The man was from Perth, Australia. He had been living in Boston for nearly eighteen years. He had come as a student and now ran a business breeding small and midsize animals. He had been a research scholar in one of the most famous universities in the world. His love for animals had propelled him to his lifestyle and profession, which he pursued with passion. He was very happy indeed.

After a long ethnocultural exchange, we descended to our woes and worries. He admitted that he was doing well and was always looking for good people to help him run his business.

"Good people. Apparently good people are there in abundance," he said, "but we like to believe unfortunately that they are either out of town or did not exist to start with."

I felt that not many people might want to be involved in businesses that used animals for research.

Suddenly he asked me what I was doing. I was glad that he was the one who asked me and that I didn't have to ask him for a job. I told him that I was looking for something to do that would sustain me while I was getting my teeth into the life and living in Boston, seven thousand miles away from my island home—a different universe, to say the least.

He introduced himself as David Buster. He loved Boston. He loved Boston's pretentious suburban, almost village-like, simple life as opposed to New York or Washington, not very different from Perth, which was as much alike or different as Sydney is to Melbourne.

He said, "I am actually looking for someone to help me in my animal-breeding business. The job is mainly transporting animals to various centers within the greater Boston area. Maybe you would like to come and visit my facility and spend a couple of days looking around and then tell me if you would like to join my company."

I had no idea what the job was about. Apart from seeing rats and mice and the occasional agouties and mountain goats, I'd had very little contact with small animals and, for that matter, had very little knowledge about how to transport small animals in an urban environment.

I did not express my joy and overriding gratitude. I simply said, "Of course I would very much like to visit your facility. Tell me, how do I get there? Should I come at any particular time?"

"Do not worry," he said. "I will pick you up this coming Saturday morning at nine o'clock, just in front of this Starbucks. I live close by; it will be easy for me to pick you up. Anyway this is on my way to the facility. I have to pass this way. I hope it does not snow this much on Saturday. At least you will be able to roam around the facility."

He departed as he came in, with layers to ward off the Boston winter.

Come Saturday I was standing in front of the Starbucks as promised. Right at nine o'clock, a huge Ford Ram stopped by the sidewalk in front of the Starbucks and honked a couple of times. I saw it was Mr. Buster, who asked me to jump in. So I did.

Within half an hour, we were on the 108 and driving southward. In about twenty minutes, he took a slip lane and entered a very private and secluded wooded property. There were no signs of any office building, big glass towers, or signpost. The truck was going slowly, when suddenly in the thick of bushes, a large cleared area and several cottages neatly designed with well-planned access appeared. I did not see any big, small, or midget animals anywhere.

We stopped in front of one of the cottages, and he welcomed me in.

There was no match for the interior exuberance, decor, and ambiance. It did not fit with its external cottage-like appearance.

"This is my office," said Mr. Buster.

A woman entered with a plate full of pastries, a basket of exotic fruits, and freshly brewed coffee. The aroma put my favorite Starbucks to shame.

I could not help but wonder. I was just a stranger from a small, poor Caribbean island. Later I understood that this insignificance was his interest. He had several other black Caribbean workers in his employment. Like blacks in the Americas, who feel truncated from their roots, the white Australians also feel isolated from civilization. They strive to find their roots, from where they were uprooted and transplanted to new land, seeking better life and opportunities, unlike blacks in the West, who were herded in slave ships from somewhere in Africa and transported west, not to seek a better life for themselves but make it for others, their white masters.

On the contrary, white Australians were shipped in prison boats from the United Kingdom to Australia in order to clean the country off thieves, burglars, rapists, and other criminals to make British life better and safer, not necessarily for the ones who were shipped out of Britain.

So what was the difference between black slaves and white prisoners in the beginning anyway?

Whichever way we see it, the feeling of lost ancestry, lost culture, and lost home pounds the same way in the white man's chest as it does in the black man's chest. Mr. Buster found a cosufferer in me and, for that matter, in all blacks and people of other color.

After we had our breakfast, he took me for a tour of his facility. There were at least twenty cottages; one of them was a hospital for animals of all shapes, sizes, and colors. I met the woman vet, who was a black American from Tennessee. There were five or six other workers, again mostly black, and a few whites also.

Then we went to the next cottage. From the outside, one couldn't tell what it was used for. It was a big, expansive lab, where several scientists and assistants were deeply engaged in developing and fine-tuning current methods of breeding rats, mice, guinea pigs, rabbits, and all sorts of other animals.

We moved through all the cottages. Each of them was for one species: mice and rats of various colors and species—all had their own breeding and living quarters and their own caretakers and valets. Every cottage had at least five or six employees. Most of them were blacks.

I had no idea of the discipline, organization, hard work, and loyalty on which the whole system worked like clockwork, even in an animal-breeding facility. This is the United State of America; this is where the American dream is born, and this is from where the American dream takes its shape and spreads across the land.

After walking for about a kilometer, we arrived at a huge shed, where scores of cars, trucks, and vans were parked with a garage and where a few mechanics were checking some cars. He called someone named Mr. Dunkirk. Mr. Dunkirk arrived—a big, happy, and joyful man in full gear, who appeared to be always at the ready.

"Mr. Dunkirk, please meet Mr. James Wilberforce from the Caribbean. He would like to help you in delivery and distribution. He has some learning to do; I trust you can take care of that."

"If Mr. Wilberforce wishes, he can start the coming week, if it is OK with you, Mr. Buster."

"Yes, I can start Monday," said I.

Mr. Dunkirk asked, "Do you have a valid driver's license?"

"Yes, I do, from my island. I also can drive heavy vehicles, covered by my present license. But I must tell you, in our country we drive on the left side of the road, and the cars I have driven are all with right-hand drive. Is that a problem?" I asked.

With his usual exuberance, Mr. Dunkirk said, "No problem, mate."

"Well, I will see you on Monday morning at seven thirty," I said, and we departed from the site.

No hassle, no reams of paper to sign, no police report, and no medical examination. It seemed to me that the job was mine, if I did not screw it up myself.

My long journey of transporting animals to some of the world's best research centers and hospitals just took off. Even I did not appreciate its impact throughout my life.

The job just came to me without me even looking for it, a gift from heaven. My life was not ready for it, and neither was my body.

Come Monday I couldn't wait any longer to roam Boston and make new friends and be a social person again, like in my island home, where I had soccer, cricket, late-night partying, jumping into the sea, studying for examinations together, and all those things one could do there to be sociable while one was still in school. Most importantly being a leader in school was my most exciting pastime; I had dreams of being the prime minister of our country or maybe an ambassador to some distant land. As I grew up, reality touched my thinking. All I wanted was to have a stable profession, to be a family person, and to help my parents as much as I could. This was not a big dream; this happens to most of us even without dreaming.

I felt that I was on my way to getting what I wanted out of life.

CHAPTER 4

FOUND MY LOVE

Every morning we put crates of animals in trucks to drive them to their destinations. I was a helper only. My job was to put the crates in safely so that they did not wobble too much during the journey or jump out of the truck or the van, as the case might be. The little animals got upset and scared with a rough ride. The animal keepers of the big places where these little souls were delivered to told us several times that it was important to have a smooth ride so that the animals would not be scared or terrified during the journey. We did our best to keep everyone happy.

We had to deliver them to many places: big university research centers, big hospitals, big laboratories of all shapes and sizes scattered throughout the greater Boston area, schools, colleges, and surprisingly some private homes. I had no idea who needed them, what they needed them for, or what happened to these thousands of little creatures.

The driver was always the same, Mr. Durant, a white elderly man with a big build; he was strong with a soft and kind voice. He said he had been with the company almost from the very beginning. It started in one cottage, but now it had more than twenty cottages with bigger glass buildings and the big garage, which housed several half-ton SUVs and buses to carry cargo. He had seen the business grow. My driver frequently carried crates full of animals to the airport for export abroad: Japan, Taiwan, South Korea, countries in South America, Australia, and occasionally to China and India. This company had a huge worldwide market, because of the purity and rigidity of the breeding and rearing processes.

The old man told me these animals were used for scientific studies of various sorts. Indeed they were used for experiments in curing diseases, discovering drugs, studying genetics, and you name it—all were used in the name of the advancement of science and saving civilization and humanity.

I had difficulty understanding how these little creatures could do all those big things. Big indeed, in every respect. Very big money, very big science, big discoveries, and many new beginnings.

"That is another story," said Mr. Durant, the driver and my mentor.

During these circuits one day, we came to a very smart multi-story building, maybe ten or twelve stories high, close to my home.

We drove to the back of the building. A guard met us at the entrance and checked Mr. Durant's ID and papers. He asked who I was and also checked my papers. He asked me to open the back door of the van in which we were carrying our cargo. He jumped up and checked each of the carrier boxes, carrying white rats only. There were twelve boxes; each had twenty rats. He checked all of them and said good luck to the little creatures. He then asked me to close the rear door, and with touch of a button on the remote control he was carrying, the front gate started to wind up, making a siren-like noise. We entered into a big basement parking hall. As we entered, we saw several red lights start to blink. Two black officers escorted us to the lower floor to the entrance of what I learned was the reception for the animal house. A young woman again checked our papers and advised us to stop in front of the third door to the right.

There was the real depository of our cargo. Two workers came and picked up each of the boxes from the van themselves and checked the contents and numbers in each container. They completely unloaded all the boxes onto a motorized cart, more like a golf cart, that they drove through the wide entrance of the animal repository. They said good-bye to us, and the huge gates closed automatically as they disappeared inside the tunnels of darkness.

As we were ready to leave, a voice came on the speaker, asking us to stop by the reception office. When we did, the woman was waiting for us and checked our delivery papers.

She smiled a mysterious smile and said, "Well, good-bye, James. See you in two weeks."

That was when we were expected to return with a new shipment, in two weeks.

"Of course," I said and asked, "Will you be here in two weeks? That will make my job easy."

"I hope so," she said, and finally we departed.

This was what I had been doing with Mr. Durant for the last six or seven months, delivering small creatures in hundreds.

The woman seemed to be in her midtwenties. She was pleasant, soft-spoken, and black, and she spoke like a Caribbean woman. I was more or less certain that she was from the Caribbean. She could even be from my island. I did not dare to ask. In the Caribbean, irrespective of the time of the day or night, people generally greet others by saying, "Good day," be it morning, afternoon, evening, or night. That was a giveaway, I thought.

I was encouraged to know her ancestry to know her better, perhaps next time. Two weeks were not a long time. She was pretty in my eyes, looked more Caribbean than African—that is, straighter dark hair rather than deep curly African hair. She was not small but slight. I liked watching her walk from the reception desk to file storage and back.

So I waited. Two weeks went by fast enough. We and the company had been busy and growing faster than the expectation of Mr. Buster, the Australian boss. In the meantime, I met him several times. It seemed that he was always happy to see me and always greeted me with a smile. He asked about how my job was going and if I was happy. He asked about my family back on the island and those in Boston.

Mr. Durant told me one day, "Nobody comes here for a job interview. It is Mr. Buster who brings his choice, God knows from where, and he introduces the person to everyone and explains the position of the new employee; then that person is a part of the team. Even the present CEO was driven in one day by Mr. Buster himself, who introduced him to each individual working here. It was no different in your case. He sees the important and vital role of each individual employee and has love and respect for everyone who works here. You will find that once they're in, very few people leave the job, unless there is a very good reason to do so."

I felt secure and happy to be a part of the company. Yet I couldn't stop thinking, where did I go from here? Would it be OK if I had to spend the rest of my life as a small-animal delivery hand? Would I be able to raise a family and look after my parents and siblings, who would need help? But I believed in hard work, loyalty, trust, and achieving my personal American dream.

Two weeks later we had a different shipment of animals. There were forty crates. After going through the intense security check, we stopped at the main reception office. There I saw the same woman, busy with the computer.

"Good day and welcome, James. Good to see you. May I see your papers, please?"

I greeted her in my made-up American way. "Good morning, ma'am; this is all I have for you."

"You have forty crates. Hmm! You need an extra hand to unload. I will ask for three people this time to unload."

"That is very kind of you, ma'am," said I.

This routine went on week after week; I started to feel at ease speaking to her.

In one delivery, I had only four crates of rabbits to deposit. It seemed to me that she was on her own and was also in a fine mood, not pretending to be busy.

I collected my courage and said, "You know my name, but I do not yours. What is your name, ma'am?"

"My name is Marina Thomas. I am from Georgetown, Guyana. Where are you from, James?" There was a genuine, kind "like to know" tone in her question.

I was delighted to tell her. "I am also from an island near you in the Caribbean. I came to Boston a couple of years ago, and I love the place."

"This is my fifth year," said Marina. "Still I miss my town in Guyana; I miss my family, my friends, and the places I used to go often with my folks and not infrequently drove to alone myself. I had no idea about Boston's cold, snow, slush, and winter. I had never seen snow in my life before I came to Boston. The first two years, it was hard, but they were excitingly challenging as well. Eventually I got used to it. If snow begins late in the season or starts to disappear early, I feel like something is missing. But I love the city. There is so much to see, so much to do, and so much to explore and learn that one does not feel lonely or need close friends here.

"I love my job. Even more, I like that there are so many different kinds of people, those who work here almost from every corner of earth. I meet some fascinating people, both men and women, of every color, shape, culture, and language. It is just impossible to imagine unless one is actually in the thick of it all. This is one of the most respected cancer-treatment-and-research centers not only in the United States but also in the rest of the world. Here one meets many great people. Many great brains, thinkers and producers, and many more ordinary folks like me."

She went on and on.

I realized that deep in herself, she had to be lonely and maybe happy to get a real listener. I did not lose this opportunity and the auspicious moment.

I said to her, "Hi, Marina! You have so much to say, and I have so much to learn; you could be my perfect tutor."

She stared at me for a second. "Well, when do we begin?" she said.

"How about coming Saturday to the Starbucks next to this office, on the left side as you come out of the main gate, at eleven o'clock sharp in the morning? Do not forget. I will be waiting for you, Marina."

That is how it began, and that is how I found my love in Boston.

There had been many visits to Starbucks and many evening walks in the park and by the pier, where they reenact the Boston Tea Party by throwing crates of tea overboard into the Boston Harbor, wandering by the banks of the Charles River, exploring Boston Public Garden, going to museums and movies, and walking the Harvard and Copley Squares in evening. At night bags and bags full of popcorn just kept disappearing while we listened to music from faraway countries, ice creams melting away in our mouth or falling by the roadside, riding the T (the Boston metro), and going nowhere.

I never knew there were so many things to do apart from cricket, football, or fishing in the streams of the island. During what little time we had during the weekend or some days after work, we stuck to each other. I filled her loneliness, and she my heart. That I knew for sure.

Once I asked, "All the animals I bring—what you do to them? Do they live here for the rest of their lives? How do you keep them?"

"Perhaps you would like to visit our holding area," said she. "We need to go through some formalities. As the breeder and supplier of the animals, you are justified to inquire about their well-being. I will ask permission from the CEO and prepare the paper work for you. I need a copy of your passport and two passport-sized photographs."

The following Monday by special invitation from the CEO, I was escorted to visit the small-animal holding facility. The animals were kept in individual cages in a clean air-conditioned facility. There were rooms that looked like operating theaters. My escort took me around and showed me the small-animal operating room, research lab, genetics-study lab, and a host of other fitted rooms assigned to perform various work. As we finished our tour, she produced a visitor's remark register and asked me to make comments on my observation about the facility.

Very strange—I was only the man who transported animals from our breeding facility. I was no scientist or doctor. This was one of the best medical research centers in the world. What a joke. I was just a high-school leaver, and I had to make comments about their standard of work.

Both Marina and my escort said that my comment would be very useful, because I was one of the main animal handlers. I scratched my head several times. There was nothing I could write except "Simply wonderful." That was significant. That was the greatness of a place like this, where there were great people and where, to them, all human beings were equal.

The day came when it became serious between us, and we started looking at the future of our friendship. I did not have to wait; she was the one who spoke.

One day she said, "James, it is time you get married and have your family, if that is what you would like."

I was waiting for this moment. I did not know what to say.

"Marina! You have a master's degree in cell biology from Trinidad, and I am just a high-school leaver. How could I even dare to propose you to marry me? I am grateful for your friendship."

She burst out laughing, which went on for some time, an uncontrollable laughter. Eventually she stopped and said, "I am not a scientist, just a laboratory secretary keeping the books and taking minutes from time to time. James! If you are looking for a school leaver from the Caribbean in Boston, you will be looking forever. Here everyone has a baccalaureate, master's, or a PhD. So look at who comes with degrees and decide whether together we can go to the church and go to the marriage registrar."

So we decided that we were to get married, and the sooner the better. We made our appointment with the marriage registrar and a date with an available church. We informed each other's family, hers in Guyana and mine in an emerald island in the Caribbean.

Soon we got married and moved into an apartment on Boylston Street, close to her work and a stone's throw from the T to my work.

CHAPTER 5

BEGINNING OF A HONEYMOON

Just before we got engaged, I disclosed it to Mr. Buster. He called me to his office, asked all about my fiancée, and got my file out.

"Well, perhaps you might like to take a different responsibility," he said. "You have been handling the animals and doing your job well. You are knowledgeable about our work and have seen how the system works. I would like you to take over the running of cottage number twenty, where we breed and nurture white rats. The present supervisor would like a change; he could do with some fresh air and will be swapping with you. You will be fully in charge. We will give you training and instructions on how to manage. Since this will be more professional work with more responsibility, your pay will be better, and some other advantages also come with it.

"You are just going to be married; you could do with some change, both at home and at work. Shirley, the HR manager, will give you details and the new contract for the job, which will start from the beginning of the coming month. You have any plans for a honeymoon? We from the big continents strive to get married or spend our honeymoon in exotic Caribbean islands. I wonder where the people who live in the sunny and sandy Caribbean islands go for their wedding or honeymoon."

"They should choose the Andes, Himalayas, or Alaska," I suggested.

"I presume it is Alaska for you," he said.

Even before we got married, we had been dreaming of driving to Alaska one day. That was a dream. I liked to drive, but I did not own a car. Marina owned a car, but she was scared of long-distance driving. Flying was not always the fun way to travel. Were we ever to go, we could drive, but that was also a dream.

"Yes, sir!" I said. "If we get the opportunity, we would like to have our honeymoon in Alaska. Money is a problem. We may solve it by begging, borrowing, or burgling. This will be once in a lifetime, and both of us are working and have steady jobs. We would like to drive and not fly. That raises the question of time. Driving to Alaska and back from Boston will require at least four or five weeks. Even if we solve the money problem, how on earth we can get one month of vacation time for both of us at the same time? Maybe we will drive to New York or Cincinnati or to Toronto or Montreal in Canada for our honeymoon."

Mr. Buster listened. "Hmm," he said. "You get two weeks of paid vacation a year. If you really want to have your honeymoon in Alaska, I will give you another two weeks of fully paid holiday as my gift for your wedding."

"Oh! Thank you, sir! Are you really serious, really?"

"Of course I am serious, with the understanding that after your honeymoon is over, as you return, your real honeymoon with work will start. You will be taking responsibility of another cottage, full of different creatures. With increased responsibility, your income and position will also change. Is that agreeable?"

I could not believe my ears, and I could not believe that I was seeing and speaking to another human being. Or was it an angel from heaven? I never thought that such people lived among us. Not only my wedding and honeymoon but also a promotion. *What have I done to deserve this?* I asked the heavens.

I could not thank him enough. As I was leaving, I said, "I can't express my gratitude enough for your kindness."

"You deserve it, James," said Mr. Buster, and we departed.

A month later we began our much-cherished dream-come-true honeymoon to Alaska. We decided to take the northern continental route rather than the southern one close to American border.

It was a memorable event of a lifetime. I would need another volume to pour out all my emotions that erupted during this adventure. In my country where I was born and grew up, after driving for two hours in one direction, I would end up floating or sinking in the sea. After driving back in the same direction for two hours, I would be hitting the foothills or dangling from a cliff, about to drop in a deep gorge.

These miles and miles of open land—be it flat, be it forest covered, be it hills and mountains—appeared to be an eternity. I never thought the earth was so huge—never-ending space, the sky, and the air. I grew up believing my little island was the world, where it began and where it ended, that we were the ultimate.

For me, this journey made me believe I was born again. Indeed I was born again, part of the universe and beyond the reach of my old little world, my island home, where my heart was, but my mind was beyond its reach, somewhere else. I couldn't imagine how I would get these two together again, if ever.

My wife and I took turns in driving the entire trek. We left Boston and went through Montreal, Toronto, Winnipeg, Edmonton, White Horse, Yukon's Gold Rush countries, and across the Alaskan border to Anchorage. Fortunately, it was the month of July. There was no snow to be seen, very unlike Canada and Alaska. When we think of Canada, all we think about is snow, blizzards, frozen lakes, and rivers, but we saw none of these. We saw snow only on Mount McKinley. I had adjusted to snowy winter in Boston. But Canadian and Alaskan winters were something else, and we were neither prepared for nor looking forward to the wintry experience during our honeymoon. Our planning was good, and God was kind.

We returned along the Pacific West Coast from Juneau, Alaska's capital, to Vancouver to Calgary, Regina, Winnipeg, and back to Boston from Toronto.

The indescribable impact this journey had in our minds, bodies, and perceptions of us as human beings needed to be recorded.

Both of us kept our own diaries meticulously and compared them from time to time. The impact of the world on us was so very different. She was a well-educated, sophisticated, well-spoken Trinidadian university graduate. And I was a half-educated high-school graduate who grew up and lived in the mountain with nature, thriving by muscle power, sparing my brainpower to brood.

I must one day tell this story to the world with my heart and soul, to share one little islander's transformation in a honeymoon in heaven yet so close to life.

We hoped that it would never end, but it did. We were back in Boston in our treasured little hole-in-the-wall apartment. Yet the smell of romance, the beauty of the music, and the passion of togetherness filled the apartment.

Back to work, back to business, and back to sourcing people. Counting bodies to hours and hours to bodies, as she went back to being the HR leader in her company and I went back to the animal kingdom.

CHAPTER 6

HECTIC LIFE

With the American dream came American stress, American bills, and the American IRS. This was the package of a nightmare that came with the dream, of which no one ever spoke to us; they never advised us or warned us to steer clear of the dollars that did not exist. Those dollars did not belong to us, except on paper. We had no idea how that imaginary money could change into real money needed to pay tax. We needed real divine help.

Accountants told me I was worth far more than what I thought. Yet I was really struggling to imagine being worth that significant sum of money.

It was five years since we had married. We had three beautiful girls. They were as playful as they were attentive to our wishes and desires. All the credit went to my wife, who was bringing up the little ones. She took the full brunt of her pregnancies, and all three were born through cesarean section. None of the cesarean sections were planned, but all had a valid emergency reason to have C-section.

I was busy looking after the business. It was growing faster than we could imagine. With success came responsibility. I rose through the ranks from handler to dispatcher and then to assistant manager and eventually manager of the unit. From there, I made enough money to actually buy the business from Mr. Buster. I never imagined that a black man from a small island in the Caribbean would ever become a businessman and own a business, a business that fed the lifeline of science—nowhere but in Boston, the epicenter of scientific thinking and discoveries, the city that kept the world of science rolling, tossing, and turning.

I was happy. I was no scientist; I was no intellectual, but I was happy that what I did for a living kept the scientists and scientific minds growing and glowing on their successes and pounding and shredding on their failures.

My business continued to grow with the demands for varieties of living creatures, from rats, mice, and guinea pigs to pigs, lambs, dogs, horses, and even chameleons.

Once a request came from Germany to procure Southeast Asian orangutans for science. Along with the request came thick, serious-looking government files giving the researcher and the research institute both legal and moral authority to carry out experiments on Southeast Asian orangutans.

They wanted two of them. The condition was that if the tests on the first animal failed, the requesters would return the second one, which I had permission to release into Indonesia's wild or to use for some other purpose, as long as some stipulated conditions were met.

I learned much about animals and human beings, relations between people and beasts, people and their pets, although I wasn't in the business of pet animals.

The bond between people and animals was so intriguing and complex. People can kill them for the power of knowledge, can live with them in the same bedroom, can sell them for unimaginable dollars, can play with them as a toy or a family, and can even sacrifice their lives when hungry or even for pleasure.

The reputation of my company was now all across the Americas and beyond, even across the Atlantic in Europe.

Once from a Swedish agent, I got a request to acquire desert snakes from all over the world or as many as deserts as I could gain access to. It was a very difficult order to entertain. I had no idea how to go about it. I did not want to decline the order.

By then I had just over one hundred men and women working with me. I had to increase the facility significantly, lease more neighboring lands, and build more animal cottages and staff quarters.

Money was plentiful, and banks were more than generous.

I put the request for the order to our senior members for ideas. One day one of the men, named Rajab, a Palestinian man working with small animals, came to me and said that he had spoken to a friend in Cairo, Egypt, who was optimistic about being able to procure desert snakes from the Middle East, Sahara, and Kalahari but that he had no access to the Chinese and Australian deserts.

That was a great start, I thought, and asked Rajab to arrange a meeting with his contact. I contacted my Swedish contacts and mentioned partial fulfillment of their order. They were very happy.

But I continued to explore and identify contacts for the great Gobi Desert in northern China, the Australian outback, and South American Patagonia.

My client was in no hurry. Eventually within two years, we were able to supply snakes from most of the world's known deserts to my Swedish client.

The surprises were never ending; a call from Santiago surprised me. I thought we were in the animal business. More surprising was that this company based in Santiago, California, asked us to supply river dolphins for research. My immediate reaction was to refuse the order. This American company had all the papers from the state, from the federal government, and also from a famous California university allowing them to carry out the study on river dolphins, no doubt an important research work. I had no idea where to get them; we had no facility to keep and store them. I had to call in an expert fish breeder to help me build an enormous aquarium for temporary habitation.

Still I had no idea how or where to acquire them. Help came from India. A fish broker informed me that Indian rivers, especially the Ganges, were the natural habitat of the river dolphin. Unfortunately, river dolphins are protected by law in India. You can't fish for them or even catch them for research. Even if we could get the Indian government's limited permission to catch a few for research, the World Association for Prevention of Crimes against Animals (WAPCAA) would never allow us to catch river dolphins, a protected species, to go under the lights of a scientist's experimental table.

So it was a futile exercise to convince the WAPCAA to give us permission to catch river dolphins for scientific experiments. But Bangladesh was a different scenario all together. No hassle, no bustle, Bangladeshi rivers are also natural habitats of river dolphins. It was unclear if, like in India, river dolphins were a protected species in Bangladesh too. Putting any fish in a protected category in Bangladesh would be political suicide, as millions and millions of people's survival depended on fishing in the rivers.

All we had to do to find was reliable and credible fishmongers in Dhaka, and the crates with swimming river dolphins kept coming until the study ended. Now that we had moved from the land to the water, the sky was the limit, but that did not last very long.

Soon after the river dolphins, we got a request from a South African institute asking if we could supply them with finches for scientific experiments. That was even more challenging, since neither I nor my wife was a bird fancier or had any experience in taming wild finches.

But we took this challenge in stride. Our children loved birds, but they were all toy ones. We found a supplier from South America. The problem was solved, or so we thought. Building a bird sanctuary was a completely different ball game than our business. There was no one better than the keeper of birds in the Boston Zoo. But the best advice and help we got came from a local pet shop, which helped us to build a reasonably and manageably sized birdcage. We also learned several bird-keeping tips from the owner of the shop. That was a learning issue we had to go through. I guess not many in my business are familiar with bird keeping.

It was going well; the transportation arrangement was satisfactory, and the institute in South Africa was highly complimentary about our level of professionalism.

Then some of the bird keepers started to get sick with flu-like symptoms, and after several tests, the doctors said that this was most likely some form of allergic reaction from the association with the birds. A few others in other areas also developed the same sickness, but most of them got better with time and simple medication.

We heard of bird flu, SARS, chicken flu, and Hong Kong flu, which resulted in thousands of chickens being slaughtered. When the sickness returned in our camp, we all got scared, and the city health authority was contacted. But they were reassuring and did not think that the sickness came from the finches. So they did not order a mass killing of the finches we had. Their lives were spared, and the South Africans continued to do their research.

We were told that this was most likely an ordinary seasonal flu, since it was flu season. The seasonal flu came and went with no problems, except for one person. That was me.

CHAPTER 7

THE FLU SEASON

My flu lingered on. It was not a continuous sickness but the on-and-off kind. When it was on, like any other flu, I had a slight temperature and occasional sweating at night. I felt very thirsty and slept longer than I normally would do. I was tired and had a lack of enthusiasm for the business. I despised my lethargy for work and like beyond any reason. But when I was off the flu track, I completely forgot the bad days this recurrent flu brought and allowed myself to be completely engaged in the business. Sometimes not even my imagination could keep up with my explosive enthusiasm for developing the business. I thought about expanding the scope of the present business and adding new facilities, and I even thought at times about building an animal-research hospital attached to the breeding facility.

There were so many different animals that we occasionally saw die unexplained deaths; that scared me the most. I turned to the expertise of reputable vets to make a diagnosis that no epidemic would erupt and conditions would not extend into the community, both people and animals.

That never happened. Neither did it linger in the community or spread in the animal colonies.

My flu never left me completely. Sometimes it was a lingering chesty cough; at other times, it was just generalized muscle ache or severe bone and joint pain, and sometimes both. They did not last long, only a couple of days generally, as the doctors advised drinking lots of fluid and taking Tylenol as often as I could, sometimes every six hours. I took the extra strength ones, citrus juices, and chicken soup. I kept happily working, especially with the extra attention from my wife and children.

I kept telling them that I just kept getting this flu, but it was nothing to be concerned about.

They told me, "It is bad that only you are suffering, but nothing happens to us."

I said, "That is the way it should be. I do not want any of you getting sick. You are the only things I have, and I pray that God keep all of you healthy and happy."

My daughter said, "Why God is partial to you? He is listening to your prayers, but what about our prayers to God?"

"Of course God is partial to me, very partial indeed," I said. "Otherwise how could I have such a wonderful person like your mom and three of the most beautiful and lovely daughters like you?"

I was overwhelmed and soaked with the passion, love, and kindness I got from my wife and three children. I would never be sick. At least for them, I would keep living and would be stronger and stronger by the day.

Quietly from time to time, my chest became heavy, and my breath short, with my eyes full of tears. Why? These must be tears of joy. I was happy that these were tears of joy and not those of sadness.

Just over a year went by, and my recurrent visits from the flu generally did not upset me. I continued to work harder. My business continued to grow and flourish.

As time passed by, I felt tired, more and more tired. I kept sleeping longer than usual. At the time going to work was a drag in spite of it being the greatest passion in my life. Yet I felt so much better when I was at the farm and with my people.

Still, I remained convinced that it was just a bad flu that kept lingering and did not want to quit. Some doctors told me that this was the nature of the disease. My family forced me to go from doctor to doctor just for this lingering flu. Interestingly whatever the doctors prescribed, within days, I was back on my feet and totally in control of myself.

I thought it would be stupid to dwell on it and let it affect my life, lifestyle, work, and the world around me. I never used big and strong antibiotics, medicine to enhance my immunity, either from doctors or naturopaths. I kept going.

One day while I was visiting one of the animal houses, the keeper suddenly looked at me and said, "Mista, you need to see a real doctor. You are not looking well; you are not looking very ill either, but I miss the sparkle in your eyes and music in your throat."

That was a man from Ghana. I kept thinking about what he said. I could never forget that "sometimes it needs a child to find that the emperor is naked." Being unbiased, half-educated, and full of empathy is just like being a child. I needed to listen to him.

I made an appointment with our family physician. He was fully aware of my chronic recurrent flu.

I told him, "Doc! This flu is not leaving me alone. Although I never feel very sick, it is going on and on. Do you think I should see a specialist to do some tests to find out if there is anything really wrong with me?"

The doctor said, "James, I think you are right. I think it is time you go to see an internist in Boston. You will see him within the next two or three days. But before I send you to the specialist, let me check you again, in case I find anything I might have missed before."

He checked my eyes, ears, nose, throat, my mouth, tongue, teeth, neck, and my chest with his stethoscope. This must have been the first time anyone had checked my chest with a stethoscope since I had come to America. He asked me to make all kinds of noises, hit my chest, listened to my heart, and felt and counted my pulse. He felt my tummy and listened to it with his stethoscope. He hit my knees and ankles and poked me with a needle. He made me walk and stand on one foot, and he checked my eyes again with a special light to see inside of my eye.

I was wondering what had made him take so long to give me a checkup like this; perhaps we could have avoided a trip to the specialist.

After his examination, I was anticipating an answer telling me that he had actually found what was wrong with me and that he was the one who could find and fix the cause of my tiredness and repeated flu attacks.

But with a big smile, the doctor said, "I found nothing that we did not know before. That is the main reason why you should see a specialist—the sooner the better.

CHAPTER 8

MY FIRST VISIT TO A SPECIALIST

For all these years of my life, I had never been seriously sick, so I never had a chance to visit a medical specialist of any sort. I had met, worked, and conferred with several veterinary specialists, legal and accounting specialists of all walks of life, and lately IT specialists, but I had never met a medical specialist, not even as a socializing friend.

I asked my family physician, "What kind of medical specialist will I be seeing?"

Since so far we were not certain of the cause of my severe tiredness, he advised that I would be checked by an internal-medicine specialist and that we would let the specialist steer the investigation, which might or might not reveal any treatable condition. They would keep watch and observe my progress.

Two days after my family physician gave me the specialist's details, I got a phone call from his office. They asked about my personal details and my health insurer's details. They said they would be calling me within the next twenty-four hours to arrange an appointment.

In fact, after two hours, I got a call from the specialist's office giving me the details of the time, place, and direction to get to his clinic. My family was happy to see that I had taken my illness seriously. I could not resist being lighthearted about it and asked my children if I had anything to take seriously.

My wife said, "Of course nothing is seriously wrong with your health, but we would like to see you happy, full of energy, and mindful about everything. You know that you feel tired, so tired at times that you fall asleep at the dinner table or even speaking to us. We have not gone for a long cross-America drive, which was your passion, for months, and we got addicted to your passion too. I loved these long trips, and I am glad that we will be on our way very soon, as soon as the specialist finds out what is wrong and what we can do to help."

My wife drove me to the specialist's clinic, which was in Brookline, not very far from my wife's workplace. She was very familiar with the area. She found the perfect parking spot, five minutes' walk from the clinic.

At the entrance of the clinic, the small but highly decorated hall led straight to reception. A smart, courteous, young black woman greeted us; after exchanging greetings, I gave her my name.

"Sir," she said, "you need to deal with some paper work first, and Dr. Black will see you momentarily."

She handed me a bunch of forms attached to a clipboard.

We went back to the lounge, and with the help of my wife and children, who came with us, we completed all the forms that needed to be completed. My daughter attracted the receptionist's attention and indicated that we were ready.

In a few seconds, the receptionist raced to us and escorted me to Dr. Black in his private consulting chamber. It felt more like a lounge than a doctor's examination room. Dr. Black, according to my GP, was one of the most respected blood-disease specialists in the Boston area, if not in the country. Dr. Black, a bright young man with a spirited stride, came and greeted me and sat beside me, more like a friend.

He asked me many questions about my family back home, me, my job, my family, and so on. Then he started to ask me about my health problems.

I told him that my entire problem was exhaustion. I was tired, which was unlike me. Otherwise I had no problems.

Then he asked me to step in another side room, which looked very much like a real doctor's examination room. There were two big illuminated screens on the wall and several wide, flat TV screens above. All kinds of gadgets were stuck to the walls. There were patient-examination lights, which looked very much like photography floodlights. And, of course, there was an examination couch and examination bed.

He examined me thoroughly from head to foot, with lights focused in my eyes and small funnels in my ears; he examined the inside of my nose, listened to my chest and belly with his stethoscope, felt my belly, hit my knees and ankles with hammers, poked me with sharp needles, and so on.

Then we came back to the lounge and sat side by side. I was trying to gauge him after he examined me. He did not look any different.

There was some seriousness in his expression, but he said, "I did not find a great deal wrong other than that you are slightly anemic. That is the problem. We need to do several tests to get to the bottom of your tiredness."

Soon after, he came with some forms and explained the various tests I needed to do. These were essentially lab tests of my blood, urine, stool, saliva, and so on. He advised me to continue with my work, as much as I could physically endure, and advised no change in my lifestyle.

I had to return to him in two weeks; by then all the test results would be in, he said.

I was not particularly worried, but I was getting concerned that if the specialist did not find anything, how could I live with this killer tiredness? How could I continue to perform at the level needed to remain committed to my family, to the business, and to so many people whose lives depended on the health and survival of the company?

I shook myself out of this depressive air, and after several deep breaths, I was ready to face whatever the specialist had to say.

I had nothing wrong; I was just tired. Why worry? I had nothing to worry about! But in the back of my mind, the thought *Why am I so tired?* kept coming back to me.

I wished that I could discover something wrong and then fix it straightaway.

The receptionist walked us to our car, which was a very unusual extension of courtesy.

CHAPTER 9

MY NEXT VISITS TO THE SPECIALISTS

Just about two weeks after I had my first visit to the specialist, a call came from Dr. Black's office saying that all the test results were now available, so I could come to see him as soon as possible. I asked the receptionist if everything was OK; was this an early call for some unexpected result? That was a stupid question to the receptionist, who was kind enough to call me to give me an early appointment, which did not happen normally, so that we could come to a decision on what to do with my tiredness, so that I could get on with my normal life.

Yes, normal life. At present, I was carrying on with my "normal" life, which weighed a ton to carry through the day—just the stupid tiredness. I couldn't talk to my family, as it would unnecessarily put them in a frantic state. I couldn't express my problems to my staff and colleagues since it would affect the total dynamics of managing the business and the company. I couldn't even think of getting someone to look after the business. I grew up with the business; I did not go to a college or a business school to learn about animal-breeding operations and effective management.

It was Mr. Buster, the Australian, who had hired me as a helper for the keepers; from there, I learned how to keep animals and how to breed them coming from different environments, habitats, and species in order to retain their usefulness, for which they were being bred. From small to big animals, from rodents to big game animals, aquatic animals, animals from faraway places, and animals from desert, I kept them, bred them, and retained their usefulness for colleges, universities, and big research laboratories all over the world. Whom could I teach? I had not found anyone who would love this job as much as I did to take them on. I should have. But it might be too late if the specialist said I had an incurable disease and that I had only so many months to live.

It was again stupid to think the worst when I did not know if I was sick at all; it was just the stupid tiredness. Maybe many people had the same tiredness and lived with it since it came and went. Maybe it was nothing; maybe I was just unwisely imagining the worse.

I had to be practical, get on with life, and go to see the specialist the next day, as he advised, for a few more tests, to be absolutely sure that I had nothing and that this was a passing phase. I would be back to normal very soon.

We were all set to see the specialist the next day. My wife, my eldest daughter, and I showed up at Dr. Black's reception. We waited at the reception for less than two minutes when Dr. Black came and greeted us and guided us to his consulting room.

Happy and cheerful as ever, he spoke loudly but in a softer tone. He asked me how I was and shook hands with all of us. We all sat around a round table. Dr. Black noticed our grim and anxious faces, full of anticipation of some dreadful news. I guess when one is sitting in front of such an eminent and internationally respected specialist, one tends to get intimidated somehow, which now I think is self-inflicted. Nonetheless, we were all worried. I could read my wife's and daughter's faces and minds, which were so deeply expressive.

In his usual charming manner, Dr. Black said, "James! I have good news and bad news for you. The good news is that we are closer to finding the reason for your tiredness. That is good. But the bad news is we are not there yet, and we need to do several other tests to find out exactly what is wrong with you. That is not really bad, since we have a real plan to work on."

"Thank you, Doctor," I said. Then I asked him, "Perhaps you would like to tell me what you found in the tests we have done. What might that tell you about what might be wrong with me?"

"Yes! James, before I order all the tests, I would like to tell you exactly what we found, where we go from here, and what needs to be done. Truthfully speaking, most of the tests are good and normal, except that you are anemic. This I could not explain by any of my findings during the physical examination, which does not correspond to my clinical findings but can partially explain the cause of your tiredness. But more interesting is that we found you have too many proteins in your blood and more proteins in your urine than normal."

I just could not resist my cheekiness. "Dr. Black," I said, "you mean the proteins that come out of meat? Do you think I am eating too much meat? Should I stop eating meat completely? That will be hard to do, but I will if you say so."

Dr. Black burst out with thunderous laughter. "That is good thinking, James, but I do not think that is the case. It is possible, but we must find out how the proteins are finding their way to your blood and urine instead of your muscles and bone, where they should normally be. If you have too many proteins in your blood from food, which is not used up at the time, we have other ways to throw them out of our system."

That was another intriguing idea for me. I asked, "In that case, Dr. Black, do you think the drainage system in my body, which is supposed to throw out extra proteins, is either clogged or is not working?"

"Good thinking again," said Dr. Black. He continued, "You know, James, the body can manufacture its own proteins too. It does normally anyway, but under duress, for example, the body does make extra, during starvation or a protein shortage. Some very special proteins that are needed for special functions in the body are also manufactured in the body and do not come from the protein we eat."

My mind was running like a racehorse. Anything Dr. Black said appeared to be a stumbling block in my racing mind. After Dr. Black's comment about the body producing its own special proteins, what immediately appeared in my mind was, in that case, the other possibility was that perhaps my body was producing excessive proteins, which were showing up in the tests.

I resisted my temptation to bother him with my silly questions anymore.

He advised us that besides these tests, we might have to go through more tests to find out the exact nature of the problem.

Again! Every word that came out of the specialist's mouth was godsent to me. I couldn't help but ponder that he did think there was a problem. I wanted to hit my head against the wall to convince myself not to imagine a problem until there was one.

I left his clinic with a request for some more blood tests and again a test of my urine. I was told to return in two days.

So we did.

Two days later we were with Dr. Black again.

This time he was just as welcoming but in a somber mood and had a kind of intrigue in his expression. Naturally I was expecting some bad news. I really did not know what to expect.

With a saintly smile, he looked at me and said, "James, the news I was expecting is not very different than what I see in the reports."

"What is it, Dr. Black?" I asked. At the same time, my wife joined me with the same question to Dr. Black.

He replied, "He has a cancer, cancer of the bone marrow, which normally can be treated. With the progress of cancer treatment, one can do many things to keep patients alive and give them a purposeful and productive life for years."

Although this was not unexpected news from Dr. Black with so many symptoms and so many tests without a definitive answer, cancer is always on one's mind. It was hard, very hard, for my wife to absorb. For the last several weeks, as my visits to the specialist continued, my imagination had run amuck; my mind had started to imagine the darkest images of life. But I kept thinking, *It is just tiredness; I have nothing but tiredness. Why should I worry about anything else?* What else could give me this never-ending tiredness and exhaustion, except the pressure, volume of work, and perennial conflicts—interpersonal and inter- and intraprofessional—that I had been dealing with for a number of staff on a regular basis? Under these circumstances, I could forgive myself for being tired and thinking of not being able to commit myself to my family or to my staff at work. A sense of deep guilt came upon me actually, for no reason.

I shook myself out of these thoughts again and looked at Dr. Black in order to hear what more he wanted to tell me, other than that I had a cancer of the bone marrow but that I would live with treatment and be almost back to my normal life or the like.

I had no reason not to believe him, especially since he was the specialist and we lived in Boston, one of the world's most celebrated places for advanced medical science. They could do miracles here in Boston.

My mind went vacant, and I kept an empty mind to hear more good news from Dr. Black.

"James," Dr. Black said, "I do not want to rush you into accepting and going through a treatment regimen without doing a few more tests to confirm and to understand your illness better. That means we need to take samples from your bone for some more very special blood tests and possibly a total body MRI or CT scan. You have been very patient with me; give me a couple of more days to finish it all."

I came out disheartened but not disappointed, knowing that he was trying his best to fix me and put me back to my life again.

I came out again with several papers of requisitions to his secretary. She organized all the tests, which would be completed in the next three days, and I was to return to see Dr. Black again on that coming Monday.

Somehow I felt better; the dark cloud from my mind and from my imagination started to blow away. We headed home.

We arrived home to see the glum faces of my three little princesses. They all ran and hugged me tightly and asked in chorus, "What did the doctor say?"

To alleviate their anxiety, I laughed like thunder; my wife stood by and listened. I called all three of them close and whispered in their ears, "Do you really want to hear what the doctor said?"

I said very quietly, "He said to come back on Monday so that he has some more time to think about what to do and what is the best to do for your dad. Of course, I have to go for some tests, which will be done and ready for him to check before I come." I whispered again, "Now it is dinnertime; let us go and have dinner. Do you all think it is a good idea?"

"Yes! Yes!" they shouted and ran to the table. All their anxiety melted away.

CHAPTER 10

MY FOURTH VISIT TO THE SPECIALIST

In spite of the bad news of cancer, my tiredness was now tolerable—still very exhausting—but I did not feel so desperate and helpless. I guessed today would be the day of judgment, and I would be given the sentence, good or bad; either way we would know which way we were heading.

We were anxiously waiting in Dr. Black's waiting lounge and expecting to be called in anytime.

It happened. I was shown by his receptionist to his consulting room. He had a somber but curious look. A man of his stature, his experience, must have faced every little, every big or not so big, unusual, or hitherto unknown challenges in his life. This couldn't be anything that he could not handle. I was very confident of his ability to guide me in right direction, through this maze of results, data, and findings, and scans and x-rays that were mind-boggling, at least, to a lay person like me.

He was not looking at me, but I could read in his face and mind that he was more than 100 percent thinking about me.

"James," he said solemnly, "as we discussed earlier, you have some form of cancer of the bone marrow, but it is certainly not the usual type. In my many years of practice in Boston, I have not seen a single patient of your type, but we know a little bit about it from scientific papers, researchers, and various conferences with people presenting about their experiences. Since I got your report, I myself have been doing a bit of research about the treatment options you might have and the person who might be best for you to see.

"Unfortunately all my research and speaking to colleagues has not given me much to go by. Yet one of my associates in San Diego, an internationally respected specialist for bone-marrow disease, including cancer, has agreed to see you to look at all possibilities for treatment.

"So I am suggesting, if it is not inconvenient for you, to perhaps consider consulting with him in his private hospital in San Diego. What I understand is that it is a rarer-than-rare case in America. Most of the recorded cases are diagnosed in the Middle East and Southeast and East Asia.

"If you agree, I would like to refer you to him. I hope you and your family will give serious thought to it. I just asked and spoke to him as a friend but did not give any detail of your reports to him. If you agree, I will send him copies of all the test results and my thoughts so that he will have a good idea about which direction to take."

"Dr. Black," I asked, "what kind of cancer do I have that is so rare? How can I get such a rare cancer? Do you think I could have caught it from the animals I deal with? Do animals get this type of cancer? If so, do people treat animals with this type of cancer?"

In my facility, we had a couple of dogs that had developed cancers; they were taken by veterinary research centers in Wisconsin.

Again in deep-thinking mode, Dr. Black half closed his eyes and slowly replied, "I do not know anything about animal cancer, nothing at all about your type of cancer, or if it happens in animals. Its rarity and its close proximity to one of the most common human bone-marrow cancers make it very attractive to research but not so attractive to physicians otherwise. So lots of research is being done, not only in the laboratory but also on human patients. My friend, Professor Hooper at San Diego University, will be able to tell you all we know about the disease and all standard and experimental treatments available anywhere in the world. Although in North America this disease is rare, with most of the patients diagnosed outside

America, a high number of cases are being treated in the United States, mostly by him. So his understanding and management methods must be second to none. That is what my feelings are.

"If you feel comfortable, I will prepare all the documents and send them to him and your insurance firm before you arrive, in order to give him some thinking time. He will be able to answer all your questions, even the state-of-the-art treatment and plans and a ballpark cost of the treatment."

I had come prepared with the idea that whatever Dr. Black decided, I would accept and get on with my treatment so that I could go on with my life, which was fractured in one way and more united in another way that had brought my family together. We were for each other every moment of life. We did not let our family bond loosen for anything and any reason.

So I told Dr. Black, "Please arrange for me to see Professor Hooper, the earlier the better, so that we all can feel relieved now we know what's wrong and how it can be fixed."

"James," asked Dr. Black, "do you have any relatives in San Diego where you can stay, or shall I ask your insurance to include that in the total cost? Well, let us find out the cost with and without the accommodation. I assume your wife will accompany you or your daughter perhaps."

I said, "I think at least one of my daughters will come with me and my wife. The eldest will look after the youngest one. There are friends who will also take care of my children. Or perhaps we all will come, at least for the first few days. If I have to stay for a long time, they can return to attend to their school. I'm not sure how long my wife can come to keep me company. When we see Dr. Frank Hooper in San Diego, we will find out about it all and do the best available to us."

If it was for long, I would have to assign someone to take up the management in my absence. It might not be a good idea to split management responsibilities, which might create conflict and mismanagement and, in the end, loss of customer confidence and business in general. If it was for a short time, I could continue to look after the business from San Diego. These were the important issues that came back and forth in my mind. I had to make a concrete decision. Of course, I couldn't make any decision until I had seen the professor in San Diego.

This unsettled mind was more troublesome than my illness. It was particularly bothersome, myself being away from home and away from work and the city I loved to live in and work. I loved to live and work in Boston despite my work having expanded beyond my city, state, and even the boundaries of my country.

I think I was trying to deceive myself by jamming my mind with all these less important issues to avoid thinking about the consequences of my serious illness that was cancer—not just any cancer but a very rare type of bone-marrow cancer. I did not want to even think how I had got cancer and such a rare cancer that very few people in the world got and few specialists had the expertise in. Even a vast, most advanced country like the United State of America, the brightest star in the world, had limited ability to handle my case. Well, on the contrary, it was not a limited ability but a limited scope of challenge due to too few patients; however, because of available expertise and technology, patients from all over the world can converge on the United States and give doctors and scientists enough challenge to solve the problem. Again my thoughts were out of control and getting more bizarre. I couldn't stop thinking. Now I would not force myself to stop floating on these thoughts, dark, depressive, or bizarre as they might be; I would let my mind be drained of these thoughts and be cleared so that I could face the professor in San Diego with an open, clear mind that listened to reason and acted for the best.

I couldn't be more grateful to Dr. Black for being the kindest, most honest, and most ethical professional, who spent so much of his valuable time to find out whatever was wrong with me and to find the best specialist in the country, if not in the world, to treat my rare cancer of the bone marrow. I felt better already with these thoughts. I felt confident; I felt I was on my way to getting rid of my misery and coming back to rule and flourish in my world again. Of course I would.

Anyway, it was time to get all the instructions from Dr. Black and prepare to go to San Diego as soon as the call came.

Dr. Black said, "All your documents have already gone. Lisa, my secretary, will give you copies of all the documents. I have sent your contact details to his office; you also have his contact details. You will soon hear from his office to make your travel arrangements."

We said good-bye to Dr. Black, took our package from Lisa, and went on our way home.

CHAPTER 11

PHONE CALL

It was late in the evening when we arrived home. The children were as anxious as ever. They were all awake and waiting for our return.

"Dad! Dad! Dad! Mom! Mom!" they called out.

The eldest one asked, "What did he tell you? Do you need any treatment? Do you have to have any surgery? Can you be treated in Boston? Do you have to go away? Boston is the best place for any medical treatment. The doctors here can do everything for you. I am sure you do not need to go to another place."

Anxious little kids! They had no end of questions for us. They were not yet sure if their dad was sick. Dad couldn't be very sick. Dad was only very tired. He worked so hard, so many long hours. There was no reason for him to work so hard. There were so many people working for him. They would be able to help. That was what Mum told them before they went to see the specialist today.

We both gave all of them a big hug and said, "We are all hungry, aren't we? Then let us have dinner, and we will plan after we finish dinner."

We tried hard not to talk about my visit to the specialist, his plan for my treatment, anything relating to my illness. We talked about the movies, the newly arrived pandas in the zoo from China, the Red Sox, and the day at school, and their homework, and we chitchatted about many "nothings." Actually the dinnertime went much longer than it normally did. I think we all subconsciously tried to avoid bringing up today's specialist's visit and the advice and plan the specialist had for me.

On the other hand, on second thought, perhaps we should have discussed the plan for us to go to San Diego to see another specialist and to be away from home for days or even weeks so that we all could have rested and slept well. At least they knew that Dad and Mum would be away for some time.

Again just the fact that we would be away for some time and that they had to stay alone for a few days while Dad was going to see another specialist might give them nightmares and wake them up at night in sweats and huffing and puffing.

Anyway we would discuss it at breakfast the next morning, which was Saturday. The children did not have to wake up early to get ready for the school and the bus to pick them up.

Saturday morning I still had to go to my office; the workers still came to look after the animals and stock. In my business, there was no Saturday or Sunday; like hospitals and hotels, we needed to care for our "guests" and "lively livestock." The vet visited on Saturdays or Sundays, as she had some free time out of her clinic. I was expecting her today around eleven o'clock.

The children and my wife were all up, slowly getting ready for the Saturday morning breakfast. It was about nine thirty in the morning. Not unexpectedly, my house phone rang. I picked up the phone; normally if the children were around, they would run to pick up the phone, because mostly it was their friends who called on the house phone. Cell phones were big, bulky, not easy to carry, and certainly not child friendly. But I had one, and several of my supervising staff carried them, simply because of the nature and venue of their activities.

I picked up the phone, expecting the voice of a family friend or one of my children's friends. But a female voice asked me to confirm the number and also asked me if I was Mr. Wilberforce.

The woman on the phone then introduced herself, "Dr. Mary-Ann Sanford. I am a research associate of Professor Hooper of San Diego. Dr. Black, your blood-disease specialist, requested Professor Hooper to see you for a consultation as soon as possible." She said, "I just happened to be in Boston to attend a scientific conference. I had a couple of papers to present. Professor Hooper called me from California and asked me to contact you and discuss briefly the purpose of the visit and give any assistance we can offer for your travel to San Diego. I expect your wife will be coming with you in the first instance; we can help you both make travel arrangements, if you wish."

I was amazed that a world-renowned specialist from a world-renowned hospital was providing such quick, personal contact. I had been just getting concerned about making contact, the consultation visit, a place to stay, locating the clinic, the insurance, and so on.

The woman said she would see me this afternoon to discuss the details of my visit and the travel arrangements.

At the breakfast table, we were all keen to hear about the plan. I told my daughters that Dr. Black had arranged for me to see Professor Hooper in San Diego. Apparently he was the most experienced and most respected specialist for diseases of bone marrow. Dr. Black, with all the tests he had done, confirmed that my severe tiredness was due to a shortage of hemoglobin, which is responsible for my anemia that is making me tired or some form of sickness of my bone marrow.

Most encouraging was that before I had the chance to contact Professor Hooper, just now I had got a call from one of his research associates, Dr. Sanford, who happened to be in Boston. What a big relief that was. We waited for her to come to our place this afternoon.

Listening to my story, the children were all spellbound. They forgot to ask about my sickness, about how bad it was. They felt comfort in the fast-track arrangements to get their dad well again.

It did not bother them if the specialist was in Boston or somewhere else.

The older one said, "In that case, Mum must go with you. We will be all right; it will be only for a few days anyway."

After breakfast, there was relative calmness. The children were calm. We all felt that a heavy stone had been lifted from our chests. We could not understand the reason for this tranquility. Nothing much had changed as far as my illness was concerned. The only thing that had changed was that we knew what was wrong with me and that someone would be accompanying me to the best specialist, who lived far away, on the other side of the country. It was the knowledge that now there was someone who would share responsibility of my treatment from the personal side. That made a big difference at home and changed the atmosphere from jittery air to a soothing breeze, even though we had not met the person, nor did we know her personally to develop any feelings about the situation.

We had a long four hours of waiting to make the connection with Dr. Sanford. She arrived right at three o'clock. The doorbell rang. We all were anxiously waiting to see the professor's research associate, who had been particularly sent by the professor himself to take care of me.

My eldest daughter ran to open the door; my wife and I followed, and then came my other two daughters. Dr. Sanford greeted us and apologized for having to have come on a Saturday afternoon, perhaps spoiling our time for rest or the time for the family to be together.

To me, Dr. Sanford did not look like Dr. Sanford as I had imagined her—an elderly, very serious-looking, and very ordinarily attired doctor, who paid very little attention to what she wore or how she looked. On the contrary, she was a very smart, young, highly polished, dark woman, impeccably dressed, who paid lots of attention to her physical appeal and sensuality. She spoke softly and politely, never in a rush, ever smiling, like a Japanese geisha girl.

"Good afternoon," she said. "I am Dr. Sanford; I am an associate of Professor Hooper. He received your reports and a request for consultation. Since there is a bit of urgency to check on you and I happened to be in Boston, attending a conference, the professor requested me to get in touch with you in case you need any help so that we can expedite your travel needs and help in any other way we can."

It was a blessing from heaven, that the best specialist in the world had sent his emissary to help me for my consultation with him in San Diego. Both my wife and I were in awe and trying to absorb this grace. We were hugely impressed and unimaginably grateful for this gesture.

We invited her into our reception room; she looked around and was uncertain of which seat to take. Her first response was, "Thank you, Mr. and Mrs. Wilberforce. What a beautiful house you have. I am hesitant to sit on any of the sofas; they all look like museum pieces, as if specially crafted for an Indian maharaja."

I could not help but say, "We were waiting all these years for at least a maharani to come and grace our home. I think our wait has been worth it. No maharani can be any more graceful than you. Thank you for coming; we are so grateful for the professor's concern and willingness to help me with my treatment." I continued, "Anyway, you are Dr. Sanford, but does that mean that you are a medical doctor or a thinking doctor? I do meet many thinking doctors in my line of work. What is a charming, heavenly, pretty lady doing being a doctor, spending time with sick people or time in the laboratory?"

She could not stop laughing, which sounded to me like music and whispering wind on the willow trees.

She said, "I am actually a 'thinking doctor,' as you said. I got my PhD working under Professor Hooper while he was in Loma Linda, California. He then moved to LA. While he was in LA, he became world famous for bone-marrow diseases and bone-marrow stem-cell transplantation. He developed his research hospital in San Diego. He invited me to join him as a research officer and also partly to oversee the business aspect of the research foundation. I have been with him for the last twelve years, and I have been enjoying every minute of it. This is the story of my life, and that is why I am here to make sure everything is looked after for your trip."

"In that case, Thinking Doctor, will you be involved with my treatment?"

"Oh, no! That is entirely the professor's area, but I will make sure you are at ease with us; will handle any issue with your insurance, medications, or any other logistics or availability; and will make sure that his team involved in your treatment understands the managerial aspect of your treatment. After all, yours is a very rare and unusual case. So we must make sure all the angles are anticipated and fully addressed—as best as can be one under the present state of the art.

"Particularly Professor Hooper emphasized that you will be coming to San Diego perhaps more than once or even on several occasions. During those times, if your family needs any help, I was told to extend as much as we can." As we kept discussing various aspects of life in the San Diego hospital and in San Diego itself, what to expect and what not to expect, she said, "Just to bring it to your attention, Professor Hooper is a chairman of several governmental and nongovernmental charity and philanthropic organizations. Since you have a very rare disease, several tests, several specialists' consultations, medication, and many procedures may be needed for your treatment. The cost may be prohibitively expensive, although he does not anticipate any problem with insurance agents. Rarely—if ever—have insurers had any disagreement, misinformation maybe, which is cleared up by clinical and scientific information.

"Under him, there are three young doctors, who are constantly looking for the best evidence for any clinical solutions and critically looking at the present state of best practice, if there is any. In your case, it is a completely different matter; practically no one in the

West has the experience and expertise on the issues of your case. He will be conferring with specialists all over the world; I know that is his style.

"I see you have a large, nice, and beautifully furnished and decorated house. I come from the West Indies. I was born in Curacao but grew up in Grenada and went to college; from there, I got a research studentship in Loma Linda, and since then, now twenty years later, I am still hovering around California. I have met many countrymen, people from the West Indies, well placed, highly educated, intellectually admired, and financially successful, but your home is very different. It seems that your eyes are beyond the West and the West Indies; you seem to find charm outside the culture of the region. You seem to have a different outlook than most of us. You still have a vast business empire, an uncommon business that can best thrive in a place like Boston. All these need lots and lots of imagination to comprehend to add the pieces together."

I replied, "Actually I was supposed to be fishing-trawler man, maybe a fisherman. It was my uncle who was a successful fishing-trawler man, who owned a fleet of trawlers and who was a well-established person in the trade. He is the one who brought me from the West Indian emerald isle, which claims to have three hundred sixty-five rivers, one for each day of the year. These flow from the mountain peaks to the outfall, just by covering a few miles from origin to the sea. My home is green forever, in rain or sun or tropical storms. It stays green and breezy, except occasional hurricanes spoil the fun in the sun. But we live on and thrive.

"It was my uncle again who coaxed me out of the fishing business. After a year of being his apprentice, having seasickness to the end of my gut, we both thought that perhaps life on solid ground would suit me better than the rough waves of the North Atlantic. I grew up on an island, surrounded by oceans, ebbs and tides, rough waves and calm ones, but I had hardly any opportunity of mingling with ships, sea, boat folks, fishing boats, or even cruise ships. While working as a rookie bookkeeper for my uncle's business, on a cold, snowy, dull, and depressing Boston afternoon, I met an Australian man in a coffee shop who offered me a job to work in an animal-breeding farm that breeds animals for scientific research.

"I took the offer. I had no idea about the work, and that is how I started. That is how I met my wife, who is actually a Guyanese girl, well educated in biological science, who was working as a receiving secretary in a major Boston medical-research center. I met her while I was delivering animals for the lab where she worked.

"If you think I am a successful businessman or that there is anything unusual in my taste in life, her hands shaped it all. From being the receiving secretary of the animal house, she eventually raised herself as the laboratory manager of a Nobel Prize–winning scientist. Her personal life has been full of struggle, but we have been together at every moment since we got married more than fifteen years ago. We have three daughters. My wife finally chose their names. The eldest is Melanie, who is fourteen years now; she was named for her grandmother, whom my wife loved so dearly that she named our firstborn after her; of course, she had my full support.

"The second daughter—we call her Satti; this is also my wife's choice. This is interesting. We knew a Dr. and Mrs. (Dr.) Pannikkar, an Indian couple; both were professors in mathematics in one of our prestigious institutes in Boston. They had no children. As neighbors from an entirely different culture, they felt so very at home with us and loved Melanie like their own daughter. We were also very close to the couple. When our second daughter arrived, when the question of naming came, we asked the Pannikkars their suggestion. They were glad that we asked their suggestion. Mrs. Pannikkar said, 'We have been thinking too. We have one name for her. We think the name Saraswati, in short Satti, will suit her fine.' They said that Saraswati was the Indian goddess of education, knowledge, and success.

"'Oh! What a wonderful name,' said my wife. 'Satti, or Saraswati, will be her name.'

"We were delighted with the choice. Our third daughter is Bint, or affectionately we call her Binta. This naming is my wife's choice. In Guyana, people of various cultures, races, and religion lived peacefully as neighbors for decades. They come from all corners of the world. One of my wife's neighbors was a family from the Middle East. They settled and integrated in Guyanese society well. From them, she learned that *bint* in Arabic means young girl or young daughter. The rhyme and musical accent of the word are charming. So she named our third daughter Bint—no hassle, no fuss. We all loved the name; we loved them all.

"So as to whatever you see in this house, nothing exists here without the touch of her genius. Even I do not exist without the touch of her finger. She is everywhere; she is the presence. I can't thank the heavens enough for bringing her to my life and for her being the absolute inspiration for all my success."

Mary-Ann was so attentive, so engrossed in my life's story, just like a child listening to a fairy story from his or her grandma.

It had been more than three hours since Mary-Ann rang the doorbell. This visit was supposed to be just about half an hour; in the end, we exchanged our life stories with each other.

"Sir," said Mary-Ann, "many thanks for taking the time to speak to me. Now that I know you better, we will do our best to make you and your family comfortable. Be reassured that the best measures will be taken to return you to your normal health. You need not worry about travel arrangements. We will fix everything for you and your wife to accompany you. I will be in touch with you in the next couple of days with your travel plans."

She bade us good-bye and drove away in a Ferrari. I realized that the woman also had good taste in life. But again, I thought, she did not need a Ferrari to make her more attractive, smarter, or more impressive. She herself would make any grace more graceful; her beauty, just as it was, would make any beauty pageant infinitely exuberant. Mona Lisa shed her mystery and smiled for real, in awe.

CHAPTER 12

THE JOURNEY BEGINS

Two days later a call came from Mary-Ann. "How are you, sir? We are ready to fly you and your wife to San Diego. Please let me know the date and the time of the day you would like to travel."

We had been expecting this call for the last two days; we were kind of prepared for this.

Mary-Ann asked, "Do you want any of your children to accompany you?"

I said, "If I had a choice, I would take all of them with me. Unfortunately, it is the school term; they will not be able to take leave in midterm."

"So they will be staying alone at home?" Mary-Ann asked.

"No!" I said. "Mrs. Dorothy will be looking after them. Moreover, I have very good neighbors; my children grew up together with their children as brothers and sisters. The neighbor's children and their parents will be there along with Mrs. Dorothy; they will be fine. We will be in touch with them regularly. They are our babies but not kids; they are all growing up with their own personalities, their own likes and dislikes, their own favorite players, singers, and movies. So they will be fine. It will be us who will miss them. There has been no previous occasion when they were without both of us or for that matter when we were both away from the children. Anyway, it is not going to be very long. We will manage, Dr. Sanford."

The flight left at noon, a civilized time of the day. Mary-Ann came to pick us up in a big limo. We had very few things to carry.

She booked us in business class on a Delta flight from Boston to San Diego. She was apologetic that she could not accompany us to San Diego, but Mr. Michael Yohanas, the chief security officer of the hospital, would meet us at the airport for the pickup. But she promised that she would meet us at the hospital in San Diego.

At the airport, we thanked each other and parted; we through the gate for our Delta flight to San Diego, and she back to the limo, to drive to her place in Boston where she stayed whenever she visited Boston.

I was thinking about the reception we had gotten so far from the specialist in California. It would be beyond my imagination back in Boston; after all, I was a patient coming to San Diego for consultation or some treatment maybe. I was no Saudi prince, just an (academic) animal handler from Boston.

Well! Maybe this was how they did their business in California; maybe on the West Coast, it was very different from the East Coast.

At the San Diego Airport, Michael Yohanas was waiting for us with our names on display. Heavily built, six and a half feet tall, fair, with a kind face, Yohanas stood out in the crowd. Having identified us, he showed us to the car waiting to drive us to the hospital. He had a soft and gentle voice and kind eyes, so very different from many security officers.

He said that he had originally come to California to join this hospital as a watchman. Then as his responsibility increased and the workload spread out, he became the chief of the security department of this hospital. He had originally come from Croatia as an immigrant. He always wanted to be a pianist or a tenor. Croatia had tremendous cultural assets, not generally appreciated by other European nations or for that matter the rest of the world. But he was happy with his job; the professor needed serious security protection.

"Oh!" I asked, "Why does the professor need serious security protection? He is not a politician or in the mafia. He is an intellectual, academic-research doctor; why is his life at stake?"

"Sir, you know that anything you have plenty of, others would like to have by hook or crook, even if that means killing the person. I guess the professor has vast knowledge of what he does. Other people want a share or to own it all, even if that means threatening his life or even getting rid of him. I accompany him most of the time when he is outside the hospitals or the labs, both inside the United States and abroad."

I was kind of surprised that the security officer of a famous professor was exposing the professor's life's risk to a soon-to-be patient. Although as my physician he was privy to all information he needed from me about myself in order to offer me the best advice, as his patient, I was not sure if I had the right to know the private, risky life of my doctor. Maybe I did; maybe I did not. But certainly it made me worried. I did not want to lose my doctor in the middle of my treatment.

However, I was quite taken aback by Mr. Yohanas speech. He was an aspiring tenor from Croatia turned chief security officer for a famous professor in California. I tried to remind myself that it was after all California, where the art of speaking was life's breath.

We arrived at the hospital. Two waiting women quickly helped us to get out of the limo and led us to the main lobby, where two other waiting women helped us to see the registration officer.

We were registered and needed to fill out some forms and respond to some questionnaires. Then immediately we would be escorted to our suites to rest and wake up early the next day. That was my hope. But we were entertained in a second room by another waitress, who offered us drinks, hot or cold, snacks, bite-size sandwiches, and some other goodies. My wife and I were still trying to absorb this regal reception. I was, after all, just a patient from Boston, who ran an animal-breeding company for research. Well, it *was* Boston, where all brainpower was generated; maybe that was what it was. But for sure, I was neither a brainpower nor an engineer who powered the brains.

We entertained ourselves with the offerings.

A smart, meticulously dressed man in a white doctor's coat came in. He introduced himself.

"I am Dr. Joseph," he said, "and I am one of the professor's assistants. I'm just letting you know that the professor will be with you shortly. He sends his regrets and apologizes for not being able to come to meet you personally at the airport."

With these words, he retreated quietly with a courteous gesture.

Five minutes later an elderly man in a lab coat, not full Californian business apparel, entered the room. He had a spritely gait and bright eyes. It was not difficult to read the name embroidered on his coat: "Professor Frank N. Hooper MD, PhD, Director, International Institute of Blood and Blood Disorders, Loma Linda, CA." It was not very difficult to recognize the man and the place we had been waiting to see and had flown all the way from the East to the West Coast of the continent to meet. He greeted both of us as if we had been friendly forever.

Again he apologized for not been able to meet us at the airport. He had two young men with him and a woman in a nurse's uniform. He introduced the two young men as both important members of his team and the woman as Sister Nora Shepherd, who was responsible for the section of "Bone Marrow Neoplasm."

Although I did understand all the ramifications of professor's institute, honestly I still wondered about the magnitude of the opulence and use of high technology in his institute. I would be in his BMN unit for investigation and for treatment as necessary.

He thanked us for coming all the way to him for medical advice and said that he hoped the journey was without any hassle and that he expected that Mary-Ann took good care of us.

"It was wonderful," I replied. "Nobody could have given a better introduction, assurance, and all-around support as she did—everything, all the way from our house in Boston to this bed in your hospital in San Diego. We already feel that we belong to the family of the professor."

"I am glad to hear that," said the professor. "That should be the way; it is what we aim for with all our patients. Well, sir! You take care of yourself. Rest for tonight, and we will start your case tomorrow morning from the very beginning—what we have done and what else we need to do, if at all anything. I am sure that Dr. Black has done most of the tests. We both graduated from the Cornell University School of Medicine in New York. He was just over ten years behind me. He qualified brilliantly. As expected, he established himself as a well-respected hematologist internationally, not just in the United States. I feel honored that I may be able to help him in one of his most unusual and rare cases.

"For the time being, both of you may stay in the same room, but it will be necessary later for Mrs. Wilberforce to go to a separate guest room for the sake of safety and hospital regulation. We will see you tomorrow."

The professor and his team departed.

We went to our room. It was just like a five-star hotel room, except there were all kinds of gadgets, instructions, safety rules, and so on displayed.

I still couldn't believe the reception we had been given, which was generally reserved for kings, sheikhs, dictators, presidents, tycoons, or the really rich, who could afford not only the reception but also the cost of treatments that went along with it.

It was always in my mind—the expense we were incurring. Would we be able to afford it in spite of us having one of the best health-insurance plans? Mary-Ann kept reassuring us that the initial cost would be covered by the hospital, along with my insurance company. I need not worry about these. She did say that they had made a strong case that I needed an attendant or a professional nurse to accompany me all the time. The insurance company agreed for my wife to be my companion in this deal. Had the insurer not agreed, the hospital's Good Samaritan Fund would have covered this anyway. I was reassured, but we all knew that the fine invisible lines the health insurers put in the agreement could be a sentence for bankruptcy. I would have been much happier to have seen something in writing.

We both agreed to wait and see.

CHAPTER 13

TESTS AND INVESTIGATIONS BEGIN

The next day we were separated. My wife had to be moved to the guest room.

Around eight o'clock in the morning, one of the professor's young assistants came. He said that, last night after they had left our room, they had had a very long discussion about my condition and the results of all the tests; they had conferred with specialists over Skype, and jointly they had made a decision to look at my case further with several other very specialized tests. But I needed to be examined from head to toe to see what they could find.

So he did. My head, my hair, my ears, nose, throat, neck, eyes, chest, belly, and groin were all examined. He hit my knees, pricked my skin, made me walk and speak and hiss, and did so many other things. He asked about my personal, social, and family life. He asked several times if I had ever had an HIV test done.

I said, "No! There has been no reason to do one, and my family doctor never asked me to get one done. Moreover, I have been married to my wife for more than fifteen years, and we have three lovely daughters." I volunteered the next question before he could ask me any other embarrassing questions. I asked, "I understand I have a very rare bone-marrow cancer, very rare indeed. You know that I deal with various animals used for medical research and I have been in this trade for nearly seventeen years. Do you think it has anything to do with my trade?"

He was happy that I proactively put forward this question. He said, "I guess that you must deal with monkeys and other primates?"

"Yes! I do," said I.

He responded, "It is unlikely, unless you are intimate with these animals, beyond just caressing."

My response was, "I am relieved, Doctor. There is no chance that, voluntarily or by accident, I may have been intimate with animals."

"In that case, that settles this HIV issue. However, as you know," he said, "there are many other ways of contracting HIV. HIV is such a ubiquitous disease; we are learning more about it every day. New discoveries are found frequently. The illness, what you have, has been seen in people with HIV, which scientists are still struggling to understand. You will hear more from the professor. He is the world's leader in your condition. So along with a few more tests, we need to have the HIV test results. I suspect Dr. Black may have done the test. I will look through his reports and results; if there is none, then we need to do the test, and for that, we need your consent."

"Fair enough," I said.

He made his notes and promised that he would return with the professor as soon as he had discussed my case with him.

An hour later, the doctor, along with the professor, two other specialists, and another young doctor with Sister Shepherd, the nurse in charge whom we had met on our arrival last night, came in.

After exchanging greetings, the professor went straight to business and asked me if he could examine me again.

"Of course," I said.

He examined my neck, the back of my head, my throat, armpits, belly, groin, and the backs of my knees. He looked happy and said, "No, I agree with Tom, the first young doctor who examined you; you have nothing to feel." Then the professor said, "Mr. Wilberforce, as you know, we are dealing with a very rare and complicated illness. I would like to do some more blood work and MRI tests to make sure that the diagnosis of your illness is correct, according the parameters set in our lab. I would like to do your bone-marrow examination again, for some very special tests that are done only in our lab. To get the results, it may take couple of days. During this time, our psychologist will develop your psychological profile, which will be invaluable for our decision for treatment and long-term management."

"No problem," said I.

The psychologist was a mature, pleasant, gray-haired man who appeared the next day. He had me go through many questions I had answered for previous doctors: my likes, my dislikes, my ambitions, attitude to race and to women, and several other questions that I could never have thought to be useful to doctors for treatment. He asked about my family back home, my relationship with my kin. Then the big question came about my wife. I had one answer: "My wife is my life. We have been married for over fifteen years. Nothing can separate us. Our lives revolve around our three beautiful daughters."

He smiled with a great sigh of relief and said, "I am really happy to hear that you have a contented family and married life. This is very important in life's success and happiness."

After almost one and a half hours of small chitchat about serious life experiences, he thanked me for the time and said that he would report back to the professor and said that should I have any further issues to discuss, I could always call upon him. He gave me his business card and left.

The next day the professor came around ten o'clock in the morning with the full entourage and Sister Shepherd. I was hoping that he would come with a solution to my mystery illness or a plan from here on out concerning where we would go from here. This was actually my wife's question that she wanted me to find out.

After we had exchanged greetings, he requested that my wife join the discussion, and she obliged. This was good; she could hear firsthand from the professor. Generally she shied away when the professor was around or during any major medical discussion, though she had proven herself to be an excellent lab director in one of the most prominent institutes.

"I think we can get to business," said the professor. "We have now reconfirmed the diagnosis made by Dr. Black. You indeed have a very rare cancer of the bone marrow. When I say 'rare,' I mean it. There are only thirty-five documented patients currently in the world, whose existence and progress are monitored by an agency based in Europe known as International Agency for Cancer Research (IARC). There may be others who are outside the radar of IARC, but not many. At present, the United States has no living patients with similar diagnoses. We had one patient, who died three years ago. Most of the cases are in the Middle East, Southeast Asia, and South Africa. You are the only living American patient with the diagnosis, and hopefully you will continue to thrive.

"The problem of your illness is that your body—that is, your bone-marrow cells—produces large amount of proteins, which is not good for you. Stopping the cells producing these proteins is the challenge. We must get rid of the cells that are producing these proteins or stop these cells from producing these bad proteins.

"There are medications that stop these bad bone-marrow cells from growing and thriving, but only a small proportion of patients respond to these medications. On the contrary, the side effects are serious, and just the side effects can kill someone.

"We have developed a system to deal with these excessive proteins, to clean your blood, and to reduce the effect of these proteins. To get the best effect, we have developed a system to keep you protein-free for some time. Getting the blood from excessive proteins is not new, but what is new is that we clean the blood at the same time to reduce the rate and quantity of reaccumulation of bad proteins. We are actively researching to learn more about your disease. The standard of care we can offer is the best and has no serious side effects, but it is done only through our system.

"So the plan is that we will extract these proteins from your blood from time to time and give you medications to see if the rate of production of these proteins is less and if they take a longer time to accumulate. Almost all your symptoms of severe tiredness, lethargy, forgetfulness, and occasional feelings of dizziness that can cause a blackout are related to too many bad proteins. After removing the bad proteins, we separate the good proteins and retransfuse them with the medications for it to work better.

"This is essentially the process, which will require repeated blood cleaning; in medical terms, it is called plasmapheresis.

"As you know, this is a research institute; if you agree to participate in our research programs, since yours is such a rare disease and almost no one has much experience in this country, you need not do anything extra, except you will present yourself for the procedure as we plan via mutual agreement. If you participate in this research, the institute will cover all your medical expenses, travel, and accommodation, and when you come, all your subsistence expenses will be covered. If there is a loss of work time, that will also be compensated. Unfortunately, at this point, there is no cure for this illness. After all, it is cancer, and eventually, it takes away people's lives. I strongly suggest that you give serious consideration to participating in the research.

"Mr. Wilberforce, Mrs. Wilberforce, think about it before you agree or disagree. Once you give us your consent, we may do the first treatment tomorrow, and you may return to Boston by the day after tomorrow."

I said, "One question, Professor. Do you think my wife needs to travel with me every time I come here for treatment?"

The professor replied, "I expect you will feel well enough to travel on your own. If you feel, or if we think medically that you need an escort and if your wife is unable to accompany you, we will arrange for an escort to travel back and forth with you."

My wife and I discussed the treatment and all the advantages that came with it. I would be under the care of the most eminent physician of the land, a specialist in my condition, and he was offering everything for free. We only had to agree to participate in the research study. Our part was to agree to plasmapheresis and the medications he would be prescribing. The only issue was that I had to be away from the company; how would it affect the general running of the company? So many people's lives depend on the smooth and productive running of the business, although I had very reliable office and business managers. My wife essentially stayed away from the company responsibility. She had three children to look after, one big household to manage, and her important job to maintain.

The next morning at eight o'clock, Sister Shepherd came with another man, who was the officer in charge of all clinical research, and he was the one I had to give the signed consent form to.

Sister Sheppard was quite lively at this early hour, and we exchanged our greetings. She asked if I had had my breakfast as yet. I said no.

"That is good since we must do the tests on an empty stomach," she replied. "Will you be able to give a decision about your consent and the information you discussed with the professor yesterday? Dr. Dover will explain the consent form. If you agree, then we can do the first procedure a little later this morning, and if all goes well, you will be on your way home to Boston tomorrow."

Dr. Dover read the consent form line by line and made sure that I understood what was read. Both my wife and I listened to the conditions and read the document well. Then I signed. Sister Sheppard cosigned as a witness, and the professor would sign prior to the procedure being carried out.

I was told to have a very light breakfast. I was wheeled to a procedure room, which was full of heavy equipment. On one side there was a recliner in which I was directed to sit. A nurse, a doctor, and another man, possibly from the lab, were waiting.

They explained the procedure to me. They planned to do the procedure for three hours this time; future times might vary. Just on time the professor with all his assistants arrived and greeted me.

"James, good to see you. This is a simple procedure, just a blood donation. But I am sure you will feel much better after it is done."

Then he gave the green signal to the team and left with his entourage.

The procedure took just over three hours, as I was promised. I was wheeled back to my room. It was one o'clock in the afternoon by that time, and we were hungry. Lunch was ready, and together we had a sense of relief that my disease was actually being diagnosed. I was being offered the best treatment by the most eminent specialist of the land. We could not ask for anything better.

We could not wait to speak to our children, waiting for them to return home from school. As they returned, we got them on Skype and told the story of our experience of plasmapheresis. It was just like donating blood, but they returned my blood into my vein again after removing all the bad proteins. This was not an uncommon procedure, and it was used for many other illness; it was more or less what they did during dialysis for kidney diseases. I felt like a doctor, being able to explain what had been done to their dad for the deadly serious and rare illness, or so I thought.

They were delighted to see their dad, not with hanging bottles, electronic gadgets beeping and twinkling all over, and tubes in my nose attached to a cylinder, possibly for oxygen or possibly for other medical gases; instead, they saw a spritely, joking, and laughing dad. Kisses and hugs all over flew across the continent. I thought I could see a tiny speck of tears in my older daughter's eye. We departed happily, full of joy and prayers in our heart.

Having had lunch, we had a quiet afternoon. We talked and talked about the whole thing again and again and could not thank the heavens enough for this grace that had been bestowed upon us.

We had one of the best nights from the time our family physician had said he would make an urgent appointment with Dr. Black just about a month ago.

CHAPTER 14

RETURN TO BOSTON: RELIEF WITH JOY

The next morning we had a quiet breakfast. I was hungry, perhaps for the first time since we had been told about my diagnosis; it was the same with my wife. As we were ready to return to our rooms, the professor and his young protégés arrived.

"How are you, James and Mrs. Wilberforce? How did you feel during and after the treatment? Did you have any side effects that you want to tell me about?"

"Not a thing," said I. "I would not have known that during the procedure they took out almost all my blood slowly, bit by bit, and returned most of it after cleaning. That is what I was told."

"You are absolutely correct. This is a simple procedure, but cleaning is the most complex one, unlike what one sees in cases of kidney dialysis. That is exactly where we come in, my clinical and scientific and general support team. Since all went well your follow-up visits, further treatments will be carried out not in this hospital but out of our larger facility in Tijuana, just across the border, in Mexico."

"Why Tijuana, sir?" I asked.

"There are many reasons. That facility is much bigger, and more professional personnel are there. This is one of the rare situations when Americans cross the Mexican border daily to go to work. Generally it is other way round. The other, most important factor is financial.

"We realize that your treatment will be a prolonged one and that you will have to fly from Boston to San Diego and from there to Tijuana or directly on US Air to Tijuana. You will be away from your business activities, and that may translate into loss of income and assigning someone to be the overseer and acting boss. All this will cost money. So I submitted a grant application for funding for your total care.

"This morning we heard that my application has been totally accepted. I did not want interruption of your treatment owing to a funding shortage. I am delighted; we have guaranteed funding as justified for five years. This is a nonprofit foundation that provides grants that support medical research only outside the United Sates. So we need not worry about the monetary part of your treatment, as we realize it would have been a major burden on you, your family, and indirectly your huge business empire. There is an unwritten understanding with the funding agency that, for this type of fundamental, long-term research involving human beings, there must be American involvement; it is better to be supervised or directed by reputed and established American investigators. As I said, the agency supports research outside the United States. There are several projects that have been funded in Asia, South America, and Africa, which are being directed by highly reputed, internationally recognized local investigators. The research does not involve human beings, or if it does, it is under stringent conditions and is monitored regularly for the ethical and human-rights issues.

"The same team who looked after you here will be looking after you in the Tijuana facility. If you liked the treatment and social aspects in San Diego, you will love it even more in Tijuana.

"What we need to know is if you will be able to come down to Tijuana once every month for two or three days in the first year, and then depending on test results and your general health, the frequency may need to be adjusted. Just to reiterate, all your expenses will be covered by the grant fund.

"Do you have any other questions or concerns? Please let me know. You have still several hours here before you leave for Boston. There is no scheduled check out time for you." The professor laughed and said, "I think Mary-Ann is here; she will come shortly to arrange your return to Boston.

"Please, I repeat," said the professor, "do not hesitate to ask any questions you might have for me or for any one of our team. You have a safe return flight home, and keep safe."

The professor departed with his team.

We returned to our rooms to get ready to leave for Boston. Both of us were in a kind of a daze, just trying to absorb all that was happening and all yet to come. It was not a small mercy; it was the mercy of a lifetime, bringing the dead to life again. We were dumbfounded with the grace of heaven.

We were back in our room, pondering the events, when the phone rang. Mary-Ann was on the phone, seeking permission to visit us, if it was not inconvenient.

Of course it was not; I invited her to our room. After all, she was also a protégée of the professor. She appeared at the door shortly after. She looked very different in her almost-military attire. I guess that was another Californian style. But she was just as stunningly pretty and attractive as when I saw her in Boston.

"Good morning," said Mary-Ann to both of us. "How are you, and how was your stay in San Diego? I hope the staff treated you and the missus well. I heard everything went well."

"Yes, indeed," I said, "it was a marvelous experience. The treatment by everyone is extraordinary, and the professor went out of his way to make me understand my illness—what needs to be done and how much can be done—in order to reassure me so that I'll be comfortable with his advice to undergo the treatment as he is recommending. The procedure of cleaning of blood, or 'plasmapheresis,' the new word I learned—the impact on me is much less devastating than the actual word sounds. I went through the treatment without experiencing that something was done to me."

"Yes, you are right," said Mary-Ann. "Taking out blood and putting it back is standard; we never have any problems with this. But the cleansing process and the dirt that comes out is not all bad—some very minute quantity of the dirt is the professor's interest. He thinks it could be good, and he wants to find out. It is just like looking for a needle in a haystack. The needle may never be found, but in the process, the haystacks are removed, as are your bad proteins, those giving you so much trouble. What is unique for you is the way that your blood is cleaned of all proteins—particularly very minute ones that are not easy to detect. This is the professor's invention, and that is why he is so respected throughout the world. It is a method that works for the rarest and most poorly understood diseases like yours. His respect continues to rise.

"There is a constant stream of visitors from all over the world: Europeans, Middle Easterners, Southeast Asians, Africans from various countries, South Americans, Japanese, Australians—you name it, people are there to learn from him.

"Aside from practicing his healing art, he participates in many philanthropic activities. He chairs and directs several philanthropic organizations. One of them has accepted our application to give maximum financial support for your treatment and treatment-related expenses."

"Yes," said I, "the professor has been kind enough to explain every detail to me so that my treatment will continue unhindered, no matter what happens, and so that we do not have to scratch the pans for lack of funds."

Having heard the events to come from Mary-Ann's mouth, we were further reassured, and hope started to heighten that cure was on its way, not out of our reach.

Then Mary-Ann handed us two airline tickets and said, "A midafternoon flight will take you back to Boston by early evening, not too late to have dinner with your children. Please check if the timing is satisfactory. It can always be changed if it is not convenient for you." She continued, "I will come to pick you up to give a ride to the airport, and one of our people will meet you at the airport in

Boston to give you ride to your home in the suburb, about thirty-five to forty minutes' drive. I do not need to tell you that.

"The nurse will come soon with one of the professor's doctors to give you the discharge notes and directions. If you need to take medication or if you have any health-related questions, the team will be very happy to answer your question."

I couldn't think of any questions that had gone unanswered. "It seems that we had far more answers from you than we had questions," I said to Mary-Ann.

Mary-Ann laughed and said, "I must give you time to relax before this long transcontinental flight and also time to get your belongings together, pack up, and dress up for a long four-and-a-half-hour flight to Boston, on the other side of the continent. Not just across—you will be going from southwest to northeast, diagonally opposite, which is much longer than east–west travel."

Mary-Ann departed, saying that she would return shortly to pick us up for the airport.

The doctor and the nurse came on time to explain to us all the discharge instructions and said good-bye, adding they would see us back in Tijuana, perhaps.

Mary-Ann was again on the dot, this time with a luxury limo. She was with us till we left the departure gate to board the aircraft.

Four and a half hours was a long flight, but as a business-class passenger, one is entertained throughout the flight. The time did pass smoothly. And we arrived safely with a smooth landing, courtesy of the pilot, of course.

At the airport, there was no huffing or puffing; our luggage was carried by the driver's assistant to a waiting limo.

It was a smooth drive return home, all quiet. Both my wife and I returned home with a deeper sense of existence, life's fragility, and hope for the future, not a concern for now. Live life for now; dream the future in the future. We had a very somber air, yet we were confident and happy to love it all.

As we entered home, the children were in some funny African native attire, dancing and singing around us, full of joy and happiness that their dad was not sick anymore and would be telling them many more fabulous stories, more than before he was sick.

"What is this, child?" I asked.

"Oh!" said Melanie, our eldest daughter, "This is a Zulu dance for the king's—chief's—return after victorious war with the other tribe. We saw a film in school a few days ago. We thought this would be the right reception for your homecoming."

We were overwhelmed. The children had matured so much in the last month or so; their love and understanding were heartwarming, beyond one's feeling.

We had changed. They were much closer to us. We wanted to hold all of them together tightly and never let them go. Oh! How much we had missed our kids, even more than the kids knew.

We changed and sat for dinner. The children were in no mood for dinner. All they wanted to know were the stories from our trip to San Diego—everything we saw, felt, heard, we smelled, and did not see but missed, being confined in the hospital for five days. They wanted to know about the doctors, the nurses, the bed, the food, and the treatment I had.

"Did it hurt?" the eldest one asked. "Did they have to put you to sleep?"

Questions and more questions, now that Daddy was back and well.

Now we felt that we should have taken the children with us. Their curiosity would have kept the doctors and nurses busy searching for answers, without getting upset or harassed. We would have to take them once, perhaps, to keep their imaginations rolling, entertained, realistically making them aware of the world and what was happening to Daddy, while he and Mum were away from home in a distant place being cured of his cancer.

We certainly planned to do so.

We were all back to our normal lives. I was full of energy, enthusiasm, and ideas, as if I had never been sick. My staff could not believe the change. That was morally uplifting to them also, as if a new child had been born, bringing messages from the messiah of a new beginning with a fuller and better world.

I really wanted to forget about my profound tiredness and loss of interest in life, which affected not only my world but also the world around me. I even had no real perception of my state of health. I was gradually adapting to it, not knowing that not only me but also the entire world around me would fall apart. I even had no understanding about how my wife felt about the changes in me, how the children reacted, and how the entire company and all the employees took the changes.

I always worked with the bottom layer of my organization; that was where I started and gradually related to the upper echelon and then to the middle and upper managers. The company was at least three times larger than when I had taken it over. We developed a serious cordiality and trust with all our clients. Including the consumers and the main business, it could be called international, but the operation and functional organization was small enough to call it a family. That was the feeling I had, a universal family working together for the same goal, helping one another for betterment of each individual personally. It was working fabulously.

I had a chill in my spine when the memory of my illness came to my mind and all the tests and treatments that had been done or were yet to be done and what might have happened if we hadn't found the professor to take care of me. Again, how could I call it a small mercy when it was a mercy that affected the lives of so many people, close and afar? It was indeed a miracle.

For more than two weeks, I had great joy and fabulous bounce. Then I started to feel weak and tired again. In the meantime, we had several calls from Mary-Ann just to say hello and to find out how I was doing. My response was always nothing less than "exuberant."

But my tiredness was getting worse; I felt sleepy frequently and dozed off in the middle of conversations. My activities were returning into a phase of suspended animation.

My wife was getting increasingly concerned. The children could see, feel, and sense the difference. They did not dare to ask, "Dad! How are you?" When I was awake, I could see their unsmiling faces. That bothered me the most.

A call came from Mary-Ann, just social and minor medical questions. We spoke for four or five minutes. Then Mary-Ann said, "Mr. Wilberforce, you are sounding so very different. Are you well?"

All I could say was, "I feel very tired, so much worse than before. I am even unable to maintain a conversation with you."

Mary-Ann said, "No worries; I am coming soon."

Mary-Ann appeared at the door half an hour later. She sat down with my wife and children. She found more about my deteriorating symptoms from them than from me.

"Let me have a word with the professor," she then said.

She called, and the professor responded immediately. He patiently listened to what Mary-Ann had to report. Then he spoke to me for four or five minutes. I was not in a real state to respond to the professor's questions. I was falling asleep in midsentence, waking up, blurting, and dozing off again.

The professor told Mary-Ann, "This is normal, no need to be concerned. It is not unusual, and it can be explained as a rebound phenomenon."

He suggested coming to Tijuana sooner than scheduled so that we could start working with him. He advised that I take some medication just to help with the symptoms.

"Mary-Ann will get the medication and arrange for your flight," he told me.

It was difficult for my wife to accompany me again, but she did anyway, having discussed it with her boss at work. They were more than understanding.

With the medication, I felt slightly better, especially I stopped falling asleep, but the tiredness remained just as much if not worsening.

The children were frightened, stunned, and desperate, seeing the sudden change in Dad's condition, from healing to hell.

Mary-Ann took the time to speak to the children and explained to them what was happening. They tried to understand. Mary-Ann's most experienced motherly, sisterly, friendly public-relations tactics made some dent on children's anxiety but not enough to stop them sobbing quietly away from me, out of my sight. But nothing spares Dad's eyes, nor his heart. I thought Mary-Ann's professional tactics would ease the anxiety of both my wife and children. That was a small comfort but a comfort nonetheless.

It was time to pack up again and take the plane to Tijuana. I was sicker than during my first travel to San Diego.

CHAPTER 15

OUR FIRST TRIP TO TIJUANA

For the first two and a half weeks after returning from San Diego, I had been reborn. Now I couldn't express how I felt. My feelings were worse than my disease, in the way it progressed before treatment. It was not only tiredness. I had constant dizziness, headaches, and nausea; I was unable to recognize people and had a very poor memory. Sometimes I was even unaware of the place or time of day. All this happened in the last forty-eight hours.

This time Mary-Ann traveled with us. With her was also another young man she introduced as Dr. Parker, who was an ER specialist.

"The professor arranged for him to travel with you also, just in case," Mary-Ann said. "He is not expecting any drastic emergency situation, but you never know."

Dr. Parker was carrying his tools, prepared to face any challenge. Though young, he gave us an unusual sense of reliance and comfort.

I slept throughout the flight with my wife holding my hand, rubbing my forehead, looking perplexed but not confused. She said she knew that something very positive was being done and that I would come out of this crisis. That was what she kept whispering in my ears. But I kept dozing on and off.

I felt that she did not want me to doze off; perhaps she was afraid that I might not wake up again. She even started to talk business affairs of the company, the great moment of the beginning. Also she told me the events of when we first met. She knew that it did not matter who I was, what I did, or where and how I lived; she would be my wife.

For months, we had met and exchanged greetings, but there had been no signs of any interest on her part that she was attracted to me. I had thought that perhaps she had believed I was a confused black West Indian man whose only desire was to find a job, a roof over his head, and a little corner to sit in and live and dream of the impossible. But I was wrong. She had indeed thought I was great and had been trying to work out a plan to get me closer so that I would fall for her. It had all happened, it seemed, without our knowledge.

I suddenly woke up and realized that we were on a plane to Tijuana.

She said, "James, you were asleep but dreaming. You were talking all about our past."

She thought I was delirious, but I was dreaming of the past aloud. I wanted to hang on to it; I did not want to let it go. Maybe I was afraid of what would happen when I was gone.

We landed at the Tijuana Airport, where an ambulance was waiting for us. Passport control and customs all happened while the ambulance was slowly proceeding to the rear of the airport to get out. As soon as we were out, the ambulance's siren could be heard cruising through the highway. It took only fifteen minutes from the time we left the airport to get to the hospital gate, and then I was whisked into a special ICU ward, or intensive-care unit.

With all the excitement, I woke up and saw the professor with all his entourage around me. He tried to comfort me and said, "James, we know now what is wrong with you and why your condition is as poor as it is."

I was already hooked to several beeping machines, hanging bottles, and monitors showing numbers, graphs, spikes, and all kind of dancing.

"How did you find out so quickly?" I asked.

The professor said, "Dr. Parker did a couple of tests on your blood on the plane while you were sleeping. He transmitted his findings from the pilot's transmission system straight to our ICU unit.

"We knew that your blood had dangerously high concentrations of bad proteins. It was so high that it made the blood thick enough to become like jelly and struggle to flow. All the funny feelings you had were due to thick blood, which stopped flowing, and that stopped or significantly reduced your oxygen supply to the brain. Your organs were all about to collapse and fail owing to reduced circulation. It was really a dangerous situation.

"I was kind of anticipating this, but certainly not to this extent, which I must say I have never seen in my long years of practice. The doctor on board was prepared to do an emergency dialysis on board; he had been made aware and was well equipped to carry it out if we had thought that was necessary to save your life. Somehow through some medical measure, we were able to avoid that and brought you here alive."

How had I missed all this excitement on board? Of course, my brain did not have enough oxygen to keep me awake to follow all that was going on around me.

By this time I was fairly awake, so I dared ask the professor, "Is it a new disease or the same one that got worse, and how did it get so bad so fast, so much, that it was going to kill me? I am sure had I not been under your care, I would not have been around to even ask these questions of anyone, even yourself, Professor."

The professor smiled and said, "James, you are tired now. A lot has gone over you like quakes and tsunamis. Do not think anything of it. You are with us in one of the best-equipped hospitals and under one of the most efficient ICU teams in the Western Hemisphere. You are protected and will have a full, healthy life back again. I will speak to you again tomorrow."

The professor left after sitting down with my wife and explaining the condition I was in. He reassured her about my condition so that she might also have a restful night.

CHAPTER 16

MY SECOND DAY IN THE TIJUANA HOSPITAL

The next day I woke up in the intensive-care unit, feeling so much better, as if I had never been sick. I had a vague memory of all that had happened in the last couple of days in Boston, on my way to Tijuana, and in the hospital in Tijuana. All of it seemed to be a dream.

What was not a dream was that Mary-Ann had been with us all the way from Boston till this morning when I woke up. She was apparently checking everything, perhaps as a second observer other than the ICU team, just to make sure that everything went right and nothing was left to speculation. I guess, in spite not being a medical doctor, she had been working with our highly respected professor and gained lots of insight into his way of thinking in clinical practice, in academic thinking, and in his vision for the future and his way of doing things. I was sure that gave her the confidence to be a second observer, and the professor also trusted her approach.

She spent lots of time with my wife, showing a real, concerned, sisterly affection. My wife was also putting lots of trust in her and felt that she was or could be a real, trustworthy friend. After breakfast, the ICU team came with papers, graphs, charts—you name it, they had it in their hands.

The head ICU doctor checked me and looked at my eyes with something called an ophthalmoscope. Apparently with this little flashlight-like gadget, they could look inside my eyes, and with this, they could also understand what was going on inside my brain. That is what the chief ICU doctor was after. He told his staff that it was all clear. There was no sign of extra pressure inside my brain. It was extraordinary that only yesterday when I came from Boston, the pressure inside my brain was lethal. Then he checked me all over. The team left to discuss me in a small anteroom. I could see through the glass window; they were going through all papers and charts and speaking to one another. Then after fifteen or so minutes, they all returned.

He said, "Mr. Wilberforce, your condition at present has improved so much that we feel confident you need not be in the ICU unit anymore. We will send you to the professor's ward, where his team will be looking after you. We are, however, recommending that you should have another MRI spectrogram prior to being sent back to Boston."

"What kind of test is that?" I asked. "I did not know that I had any brain problem. I thought my disease was that of the bone marrow."

"We did one just after you arrived. It indeed gave us the real picture of how your brain was functioning. At one point the neurosurgeons were contemplating doing a craniotomy, making a hole in your skull to relieve the pressure. But with the superdialysis and medical treatment, we were able to reduce the pressure fast enough that you did not have to undergo an emergency craniotomy. The professor may wish to do a PET-CT scan to detect any functional defect you might have and, if so, the exact location and the extent of the damage. After the MRI spectrogram, you might not need the PET-CT after all."

A little later I was wheeled to the professor's ward, a very comfortable room, which could even beat the rooms of a five-star or even a seven-star hotel.

I was very confused and totally puzzled about what my real illness was. Was it bone-marrow cancer? Was it thick-blood disease, or did I have problems with my brain? How could all these be linked together? I might have been told, yet I was confused. Nothing made any sense.

The important thing was that I was feeling so well, almost back to normal. Yesterday I was dying. Today I could be dancing. The miracle of modern medicine, I guess.

I did not want to talk too much about my feelings to my wife, just to lessen her anxiety.

Here in this room, another set of nurses checked me; another set of doctors examined me. All had signs of relief on their faces. I did not dare to ask any questions. We were all waiting for the professor's visit.

The professor did arrive after half an hour.

This time he was smiling and not worried and anxious looking like yesterday. Along with his entourage, Mary-Ann was also more or less in the front row. He checked my notes, checked my papers, and confirmed all in the computer screen. Then he actually examined me with another ophthalmoscope. He was happy to say that all the signs of pressure in my brain were gone.

He said, "We will repeat your blood- and urine-protein examination and MRI spectrogram before we can make a decision to send you home. All these tests will be done today, and hopefully you will be ready to return to Boston tomorrow or at the latest by day after tomorrow."

"Professor," I said to him, "I want to ask you something about what happened to me this time. The day before yesterday I was dying, and today I am fit, not only for ballroom dancing but also for Bollywood dancing. That is how I feel."

"That is great! I am delighted to hear from you how you actually feel. What happened to you in recent days is a very complex phenomenon, not unknown to the medical-scientific community. One can see similar phenomena in allergic conditions; for example, some allergens can give minor reactions to some people, but to other they can give violent, major life-threatening conditions. Like a peanut allergy can give minor transient skin bumps to instant death. It is how the body reacts to the peanuts that determines the degree of sickness. In your case, I presume it is not the body but the bone-marrow cancer cells that reacted to the removal of the proteins they are producing. The level of proteins and the degree of protein production rate by the bone-marrow cancer cells are at a balance—changing all the time, yet they remain balanced.

"By removing the proteins produced by the bone marrow, the cancer cells lose that balance and work in overdrive to maintain the balance. The many reasons why and how that balance is maintained are still unclear, but it happens in agreement with both the body and the bone-marrow cancer cells.

"What happened in your case is that as soon as we took the proteins from your blood, your bone-marrow cancer cells went into superoverdrive production of the same proteins that had been removed in order to catch up, but they erupted like a volcano. Normally our body can handle these undesirable proteins produced by any cancer cells; for that matter, the body can handle even harmful proteins produced by cancer cells or through any undesirable process. Unfortunately, the body can destroy these proteins at a certain pace. When the production far outpaces the destruction, various degrees of accumulation happen in the blood, which results in many serious side effects, even death, which is the phenomenon we could be facing in your case. What makes a cancer erupt violently after removal of its product from blood and others just ooze away in a sleepy fashion is unknown.

"I feel this specific reaction you had is unique to your type of bone-marrow cancer, because our worldwide experience is limited and perhaps no one treated cases like yours with planned plasmapheresis. Even if someone did, any reaction must have been undocumented.

"You did suffer a lot, but we did learn even more about your disease. What I feel is that, by repeatedly provoking your type of bone-marrow cancer, we may be able to make them exhausted and eventually send cancer cells to hibernate or leave them to die of overwork and exhaustion.

"For example, a boy unhappy with his toys, who has several boxes full of toys and yet wants more and demands to his dad that he must get him some more toys. The dad keeps listening to the child but never gets him any more toys. Having no response to his demand, the child gets more agitated and throws one toy at his dad. Having no further response from the father, he goes on to fetch another box of toys and starts throwing more toys at the dad and screaming; with no response from dad, he throws another box of toys. No response—another box of toys. And two more boxes of toys, then three more boxes of toys at one go, until he exhausts all twelve cartons of his toys by throwing them at his dad and is left with no more boxes to throw. Now the child has no more toys to throw, and he is exhausted and goes to sleep.

"We are hoping we will also be able make your bone-marrow cancer cells exhausted and lead them to death. This sounds simple, but the process is yet to be found; in the meantime, we just continue to clean your blood of the bad proteins and make you feel better and healthy."

"Professor, can this type of 'volcanic eruption' happen again after my future cleansing?"

"Yes," he said. "But this is the only way for us to keep you going and eventually get the bone-marrow cancer cells to die of exhaustion. We are now prepared to handle it if this happens again. The chance is there, but it is impossible to predict what might happen after future cleansing.

"We will have our Boston team ready and equipped. Doing the treatment in Boston is not recommended, unless it is lifesaving. James, as we said, we will cover you all the way and take every precaution that it does not happen again. If it does, we are ready to fight and win."

"Thank you, Professor, for alerting me that this might happen again. We will be prepared too."

The following day I had the tests carried out, as the ICU doctor and the professor ordered, and MRI spectroscopy tests were almost normal. My blood-protein level also came down to normal.

So I was discharged from the hospital the next morning.

As usual Mary-Ann arranged for everything and accompanied us right to our door steps in Boston. By the time we arrived at home, it was already evening. Mary-Ann took her parting hug from my wife and all three children and shook hands with me.

The children were less joyful this time, but they were delighted to see their dad like a normal person, as their dad again.

CHAPTER 17

MY THIRD VISIT TO TIJUANA

As we returned, miraculously I was back in my normal form. Back to work, back to the business of client meetings, meeting with the senior staff, and having coffee with my junior staff. All looked well and was functioning normally.

No headache, no confusion, no giddiness, no slurred speech—nobody could tell that just a few days ago, I was about to die owing to dangerously thickened blood, because of angry bone-marrow cancer cells that went on overdrive, spitting proteins into my system, making my blood like jelly so that it had difficulty in flowing normally and starved my brain and body of vital oxygen and also made it very slow in eliminating normal body waste through the kidneys. I thought I had got it right, and I was grateful to the professor for so clearly explaining in layman's terms.

"Did I get it right?" I asked Mary-Ann one day.

"Absolutely you did, James. Your clear understanding makes our work so much easier and the results so much better."

As the days went by, I started to forget how sick I was after my first cleansing. We were warned that similar episodes might occur, but prevention and treatments were just around the corner. Dr. Parker came with Mary-Ann with a doctor's bag on the sixteenth day, took my blood for protein level, and checked my system thoroughly.

Almost instantly he was able to tell that my blood-protein level was higher than before, but it was not indicating any danger. I would do the same test for the next three days; hopefully there would not be any deterioration of my health. I did not think so.

After three days of tests, Dr. Parker indicated that we needed to return to Tijuana soon. He had been in discussion with the professor regularly, and he reassured me that we should go back to Tijuana to have my blood-cleansing ritual soon in order to stop me from going into a stupor again.

As the words fell out of Dr. Parker's mouth, Mary-Ann again showed up.

She said, "I got a call from the professor to arrange your visit to Tijuana."

That was day twenty-three after my second cleansing; I was to return on day twenty-eight after my last eruption.

Anyway, we went. This time my wife could not come because of her commitment to work. Only Mary-Ann and Dr. Parker were my escorts to Tijuana. I felt lonely and alone without my wife with me. But life can't always be dictated to suit one's pleasure.

I was back in Tijuana, back under the protection of the professor and his engaging team.

The same routine, same everything; I felt better even before I got worse.

The professor came late in the evening, greeted me, and said, "You see, James, as I predicted, the same condition, same eruption may happen again. Our monitoring plan has worked; we were able to rescue you by evacuating soon enough and stopping the protein eruption. We know now for sure the cause of your first episode and the most likely culprit. It is your bone-marrow cancer cells.

"Unfortunately, unlike many other cancers and other cancers of the bone marrow, there is no chemotherapy or medical treatment that works against your type of bone-marrow cancer. Our plan to exhaust them to death might work. The good thing is that we are not introducing any poisonous chemicals or toxins or vaccine or radiation to treat; we're simply making them angry by removing their ammunition from the body and making them work harder to restock and cause havoc. Eventually their ability to restock is also diminished, and they surrender and die.

"I guess tumor exhaustion may not be a unique phenomenon to your type of cancer; it is the speed and the violent eruption that is most likely unique to your type of cancer. As they say, you can make a lazy horse run, but never a tired horse stand. Take the food away from it, it will die."

The professor seemed to be amused by his explanation.

I was amazed at the explanation, at the way that such a serious illness might have such a simple explanation. I kept pondering; my wife kept wondering, and we both kept praying.

On this visit, nothing was different, but I had several visitors in all kinds of attire. Some I could understand, some barely, and some not at all. Some only said hello, some only smiled, and some said, "Hello, Mr. James, how are you? How are you feeling?" Some just kept staring at me as if I were a 3000 BC Egyptian mummy. Some said good-bye, some wished me well, and some just turned around and disappeared.

What a fascinating world!

CHAPTER 18

MY STRANGE VISITORS IN TIJUANA

The next morning the professor and Nurse Campbell came to visit me without the entourage. We exchanged greetings. He had the hospital files and some papers in his hand. He felt my pulse and asked me to show my tongue and checked my eyes and skin all over with a sigh of relief.

"You are so much better this time after your treatment, James. Now we know well how to handle your case—the best way it ought to be."

The professor left and just before leaving said, "James, we would like to introduce you to some of the world's best minds on your disease; I hope it is OK with you."

"Of course, Professor. It will be my privilege. I will do my best to give the information they want from me."

"Thanks, James." The professor departed.

Mary-Ann entered. "Good morning, James. I trust you had a good and restful night."

"Indeed," said I.

"James, the professor just mentioned to you that he has invited some of the world's most renowned scientists to meet and speak to you, at their request. I trust it is OK with you.

"Since you are a unique individual," she said, laughing, "your illness makes you more 'one of a kind' than the others. Many scientists would like to hear your story and the way you are faring in our system. Over the next two days, there will be visitors to see and speak to you. Most of them are internationally recognized scientists and doctors, and some of them are concerned relatives of patients who would like to learn from your experience. You need not discuss with them details of what is being done here for you. Just introduce yourself, and give them an idea of who you are, what you do, how your illness started, and how you felt before and after your treatment.

"That means you will have to stay here for a couple of more days, while our guests make their way into our hospital. We will certainly look after you for this inconvenience, and you will be adequately compensated for your time and agreeing to speak to the visitors."

Mary-Ann departed after a strong squeeze of my left hand.

At eleven o'clock in the morning, the phone rang. On the other side, Mary-Ann said, "James, Professor Ian Hodson from Zambia is visiting us just to say hello to you and see how you are doing. Is it OK to bring him to your room now?"

"Yes, Mary-Ann. I am ready."

An elderly, white-haired white man entered with Mary-Ann. She introduced him as Professor Hodson from Zambia. Professor Hodson introduced himself and said that he was from the University of Zambia in Harare and was an immunologist who had first come across a case like mine while researching HIV-AIDS.

He said, "This unfortunate young man was diagnosed with AIDS; in fact, that was not the case. Eventually at the university hospital in Johannesburg, his diagnosis was confirmed to be something like yours. Since then, there has been lots of interest to link or unlink these illnesses. It is rare, as we know, but who knows how many cases go undiagnosed or are diagnosed and treated like AIDS."

I said, "Professor Hodson, I want to tell you that was what my family physician in Boston suspected, but umpteen times, after umpteen questions, my GP and the hematologist in Boston did the test and failed to confirm that I had AIDS, but still my illness is due to a defective-immune-system disease or some sort of disease affecting my immune system. Eventually my hematologist, who made the diagnosis, sent me to our professor in San Diego. I feel so much better with his treatment."

Professor Hodson asked a few personal questions about my place of birth, my job, and my family, and then he thanked me and departed with a sense of gratitude.

A couple of hours later, a call came from Mary-Ann again, this time requesting to introduce a visitor from the Middle East.

Entered Mr. Hafez Amir.

He was a tall, slim, handsome-looking man in strange clothes. Like an Arabic prince, he was covered from head to foot by a flowing garment of expensive-looking white silky material. He greeted me in perfect English and asked how I was feeling today.

He was very polite and refrained from asking questions and said, "The professor is such a highly respected doctor in his country, in the region, and internationally. I could not resist coming to see one of his most rare and most difficult cases, and I am so happy to see you are doing so well.

"We wish you well and hope you return to your normal life soon."

He said good-bye and departed. It was a much shorter conversation than with Professor Hodson.

Mary-Ann reentered and asked, "James, how do you feel about these interviews? Will you be willing to see a couple of more people today?"

"Of course, Mary-Ann. I feel energized. Please bring them in."

"In that case, I will see if I can locate the gentleman from Brunei. I will call you soon."

Soon enough she called me to ask permission to introduce the man from Brunei.

Entered Mr. Milan Darusalami with Mary-Ann.

Mary-Ann said, "Mr. Darusalami is a businessman from Brunei who is interested in knowing about you and wants to know how he can help you and other patients like you. Of course, our professor is the best person to help and guide him. He just wanted to say hello to you and wanted to wish you well."

Mr. Darusalami wore his national costume, all heavily brocaded with what seemed to be gold thread. He just smiled and greeted me in barely understandable English and said good-bye (*Khudd bhaii*) and exited the room, facing me all the way to the door. An interesting custom it was.

The next call came for another interview with a Japanese scientist.

Professor Fucohara Oguchi entered with a young Japanese woman. The woman introduced herself as Dr. Sharon Na, a junior doctor in this hospital, a Japanese American born and educated in the United States and who spoke Japanese very well. She was Professor Oguchi's escort and interpreter. I had never come across such a tall Japanese person. Professor Oguchi bowed several times with a smile. He asked several personal questions and went to the anteroom to discuss with Dr. Na. After fifteen minutes, both returned and thanked me for the opportunity to review my case. He was amazed at how well I was doing with the treatment from our professor.

Over the next three years, I had visitors from Russia, Australia, India, Argentina, Iran, Indonesia, other African nations, and several European countries. I couldn't even remember them all.

Since I was well and had met several people as arranged by hospital management, the doctors thought I could be discharged to Boston and stay under the supervision of Dr. Parker between treatments.

So I left the hospital and was soon on board a Delta Airlines flight, nonstop to Boston. This time Mary-Ann came with me, and we sat together and chatted away the four and a half hours of the flight as if we had been on a holiday and were returning home.

She again came up to our house; the whole family was waiting and greeted us, cheered us, and welcomed us in.

Mary-Ann left soon after with the promise to see us soon.

CHAPTER 19

THE NEXT THREE YEARS

Gradually I started to get used to my trips to Tijuana every three to four weeks. Every time I returned from my blood-cleansing treatment, since I had agreed to participate in the professor's research program, I received a check amounting to $30,000 to $50,000 as a compensation for the loss of my workdays in Boston. That was a large amount of money, even for us, and we were running a business whose annual clear income was $2 million to $3 million. It was a large and unusual business establishment. I kept it as a family business and did not accept any partners or investors. I did have a regular flow of individuals wishing to invest in my business without looking for or advertising for investors. Boston was the most suitable place for my business, as Boston was the home of Harvard, MIT, Tuft, Boston University, and many other internationally reputed research centers, and Highway 128 was the home of many IT, pharmaceutical, and electronic neophytes, whose numbers were growing. To incorporate the biological aspect, many of them required animal-experimental units. Although there were other animal-breeding facilities in and around Boston, I was hugely blessed to have succeeded in securing a large portion of the business. That indeed made me many friends and many more enemies as well.

Every time I returned from Tijuana, for the first two weeks, I felt great and wanted to go back to my office and look after my people, those who were devoted to me, and the business and our animals.

After the first two weeks, my energy slowly started to wane. Dr. Parker came at that time. He regularly did my blood test and decided when I needed to go back to Tijuana for treatment, which usually occurred every three to four weeks. On a few occasions, I had to return just two weeks after my previous treatment, apparently because of the fast increase in my blood-protein level. On rare occasions, it was extended to five weeks, but never more than that.

As time went by, although the treatment gave me a temporary but highly needed feeling of well-being, my immunity was slowly getting weaker and weaker. It was only realized since I kept getting the recurrent flu, occasional gastroenteritis, blistery sore mouth from time to time, skin rashes, and sore throat due to thrush. But I continued with the treatment, since that was the best available anywhere in the world and I had the best man one could find in any country. I had no reason to complain. Moreover, the hospital and the research institute looked after me very well personally, family-wise, and financially. No one in my position could be luckier.

Things were changing; Mary-Ann was getting more and more involved and spent more and more time with me. She accompanied me on most of my trips back and forth from Boston to Tijuana.

The first year was OK. I generally felt well after returning from my treatment. But the four-week break became more like three weeks. I did not mind; I was fully compensated from all aspects, health-wise and financially, and more personal attention from Mary-Ann did make me feel more confident about life. After all, she was a highly qualified scientist in her own right and had been intimately associated with the professor for years.

We were a strong family. We sincerely loved one another so dearly that we thought we were indeed one soul in five different bodies. We were happy together if any one of us was happy, and at the same time, we cried together if any of us had reason to be distressed. It was my wife who indeed kept the spirit alive and growing as time passed.

My illness did make everyone hurt in the beginning. We all cried, some with tears, and others without. After the first three months of my illness, all three children did poorly in school and got poor grades on examinations. That was the time when we were the closest to one another. All three reassured me that Daddy would not be suffering anymore because of their poor performance in school. That was one medicine we had in our hands; all three sat around and promised while holding my hand and my head and the youngest lying on my chest.

My wife grabbed all three together and hugged and kissed them unendingly and said, "Our three jewels, our three princesses, the gift we got from God—nothing can be better than these three fairies."

My wife would come and sit down with me after a hard day's work, even when I was well after my treatments. The children would come back from school and jump on my bed.

"Daddy, how was your day?" the eldest one asked without fail every day after school.

They wanted to bring drinks, tea, coffee, even hot chocolate, cookies, cakes, biscuits, candies, and many other things that made their dad feel a wee bit better. They told stories from school about the teachers, some funny boys, and girls in their classes with no end to the stories.

Some days Mary-Ann would join us, just to find that the spirit of this family was still alive, well, and thriving.

The first year went by happily with hopes of life returning to normal. We all believed it would. And we would indeed be running, jumping, singing, and dancing together. My eldest daughter seemed to be a well-trained horse rider and took several trophies for a horse-jumping competition for teens in Massachusetts.

I said, "Do not give up your hobbies; I think hobbies make someone perfect—of course, with practice included."

When I was sick or unwell, nurses would come to look after me, as arranged by Mary-Ann and Dr. Parker. Gradually Mary-Ann took over the role of nurse; anytime I needed help, she was there. I knew she was not a medical person, but again after her being with the professor for nearly twenty years, I guess she had started to understand the patient's needs.

One day I asked her if she regretted or missed not being a doctor, since she was doing so well.

"What I see are the hands of a superb nurse, superb doctor, and a superb caring and care-giving soul," I said.

She roared with laughter and said, "I hope you are right, James, and also I am not sure if I could do it for everyone."

I asked, "Why, Mary-Ann? You are capable and good with patients."

"Well," she said, "I hope you are right. But I am really a scientist, and you are so special."

She looked away.

I could not understand exactly what she meant and what she was trying to say.

The first year was really good; we all felt good. The professor frequently commented that we were about to tame the beast in my bone marrow and hopefully kill it one of these days. He really meant what he said. Well, in an eternal darkness of a night of the new moon, a glimmer of a falling meteorite can enliven the darkness with a spirit of hope and joy.

The professor's enthusiasm was infectious. It was difficult not to be touched by his overwhelming morale- and spirit-boosting words of wisdom that enchanted one's thoughts and vision. So that did it for me.

Every time I met the professor, I came out thinking and saying to myself, "James! This is life; this is not the time to give up or give in. Better and brighter days are just around the corner, so keep steady, be bold, and keep living."

No matter what happened, the professor's words always resonated with me and made me wake up and dream of the future. Now thinking back, I felt his words had the same effect, if not more, to kindle my zest for life, as his treatment of blood cleansing, which he was doing for me so frequently. But I must give credit to both; they worked together like knife and fork.

Thus life went on; at least that is what I thought. I was completely blinded by the overwhelming kindness and concern extended to me by Mary-Ann, the professor, and the members of his entire team, both at the hospital and in his research group. The financial support I was given was a financial windfall, but I could have survived from my business income, at least during the earlier phase of my sickness when the business was going full swing. But during the later phase, as business started to show lower and lower income and eventually losses, the handout from the hospital became an essential part of the survival of the well-being of my family and all the beloved possessions I had.

CHAPTER 20

MARY-ANN THE SAVIOR

Although the professor's treatment kept me alive and going, from the third year of my illness, I had a feeling that perhaps I was slowly but surely failing. One would expect ups and downs for rare and perhaps-incurable disease like I had. I had to be grateful for the professor's insight, vision, and meticulous attention to my overall health, both of my body and my mind. He asked me about my family, my wife, and my children, about how they were coping with all this irregularity and disturbances in my family dynamics. His foundation had always been more than gracious in attending to my financial needs. My loss of income compensation could be as high as $80,000 to $100,000 per month, if I had to make two visits in one month, as well as Mary-Ann's absolute attention to my daily personal health, my diet, my daily physical activities, and my psychological support. It was not only me but also my family. They took care of them, at least from a distance, so that they did not feel threatened because of the excessive attention or intrusion into our private life.

Frequently for medical problems, she would seek help from Dr. Parker, a registered dietician, a physiotherapist, and a psychological counselor in order to make sure nothing was left unattended for maintaining my health. I kept myself fit enough to travel anywhere and at any time as directed for my treatment and tests when advised by Dr. Parker and the professor.

With time, we started to become comfortable with this cyclical arrangement. All seemed to be running like clockwork.

The frequent visits to Tijuana and the visits by Dr. Parker, the physiotherapist, and other assisting professionals consumed a large portion of my time, from the time I woke up to the time I went to bed. Initially Mary-Ann would stay till the evening when she was in Boston. With passage of time, expecting some serious medical condition to crop up, she stayed behind till midnight and later spent the entire night for me. She stayed in the guest room next door. In the morning, we checked in with my wife as she was getting ready to go to work and helped getting the children ready to go to school.

Another problem we all had in mind, as the professor kept reminding me every time I went, was to avoid crowds and avoid the environment of my animal-breeding facility, for the fear of getting any kind of infection. Any infection that I caught would be a lot harder on me than on any other person who did not have my kind of illness.

So eventually by the end of second year of my illness, I completely stopped going to my own office, visiting the breeding facilities, and importantly all my important clients in Boston, the rest of the United States, and outside the United States. I was very concerned about the impact it would have on my staff and the entire organization.

But Mary-Ann and Dr. Parker insisted that I must not worry. My senior staff were very capable, and they were the ones maintaining the strength and morale and, in the end, the business of the farm.

During the latter half of my second year of illness, I hardly went to my office and discussed important issues with the general manager, who happened to be a vet with lots of experience in practice and in pharmaceuticals and veterinary research. When the visits to my office were discouraged by Mary-Ann and Dr. Parker, the general manager would come and meet me in my house with the chief accountant.

During that time, all seemed to be stable; there was no significant growth and no significant loss in the business either. They both suggested that we could very well sustain ourselves for a year without having to cut staff. But after a couple of months, they had to come in to see me wearing protective gear to protect me from any infection. These meetings were getting more and more difficult.

But it was important that I was informed of the standing of the business and also that of the staff and all animals in the sites. Then eventually we started to discuss on Skype. That way it was more direct and intimate. With the passage of time, the Skype interviews were also getting less frequent, and my contact with my people was also getting less and less.

I felt it was inevitable that, with my alleged condition, eventually I would lose control of my establishment and my entire life's effort; my blood and sweat would be going down the drain. My main worry, and a very serious one, was, how would I look after my family? Although my wife had a full-time, well-paid job in a reputable institute, she would not be able to sustain herself well. Most important were the children. How would their education, medical, personal needs, and various extracurricular activities be maintained?

I worried about all the staff, who had worked with me for years, and their family. I had very few quitters and even fewer who needed to be let go owing to inappropriate behavior. We were indeed a large extended family. We had Christmas parties together; we had Thanksgiving dinners together and many more social events where we socialized. I had a very good idea about the lives of most of my employees.

Our secretaries never forgot to send birthday cards and congratulation notes at work anniversaries to all employees and their families. At the end of the financial year, we could pay reasonable gratuities to each employee. We very rarely had any complaints from any of our employees about work or any financial or interactive sociocultural disputes; if it did occur at any time, I took the issue in my hand and went as far as needed to resolve the dispute to each party's satisfaction. I did feel proud that, in my thirty-plus years of running the business, there had been no allegation against the company for abusing an employee's rights.

Disruption of this happy, well-knit work family gave me nightmares from time to time.

Then the animals that we were trusted to look after had to be living in a healthy and generally happy environment. Avoiding crowding and irregularities in meal distribution and the quick and early spotting of any sickness had been among my most important administrative routines.

Once any animal was suspected to be sick, it was immediately isolated, and then the vet was called. We took advice from the vet—anything from returning it to its original colony, starting medical and supportive treatment and keeping it isolated until we got the clearance from the vet, or even culling the animal by incineration, for protection of the rest of the colony. For that matter, it was for the protection of the entire holding. I recruited a trained vet's assistant to do this very important inspection on a daily basis and to report to me.

Getting a colony infected is the worst thing that can happen in our kind of business. So I had the top invigilating priority to see that this did not happen. Unfortunately, even gossip about colony infection spreads like a wildfire, and clients get worried. We invited regular inspections from clients and from government bodies in order to ensure that we were maintaining the best possible environment for the animals in our custody. A couple of times, we had visitors from South Africa and Japan to see our facility.

Our business activities grew fast and farther spread out than I had ever dreamed of. My hope had been to become a deep-sea fisherman, and my dream had been to be the captain of a fishing trawler sometime in life; that was the best I could have aspired for. Getting into animal breeding was an act of God. I had no hand in it. If the support did not come from heaven, how could I have been running one of the biggest and reputedly best animal-breeding outfits?

The only encounters I had had were mostly with domestic animals like cows, bulls, goats, pigs, cocks, hens, and rarely an agouti crossing the street, deep green iguanas to the way side. With gutter snakes, no matter how innocent they were, I always got goose bumps. I never had any trust in any snake, harmless or not. Of course, there were the house lizards, mice, rats, and cockroaches, but I never touched them.

I can say again and again, my conversion from a detached animal watcher to an animal breeder had to be an act of God. And in God, we trusted.

One morning Mary-Ann came to see me. She looked sad and depressed, far from her normal exuberant self. She said to me, "James! I have serious news for you."

I was surprised and asked, "What has happened, Mary-Ann?"

I waited for her response.

She said, "James, they have found three sick animals in rat colony number seven; they are the Sprague Dawley strain."

I was surprised. They said that all three had similar conditions. In fact, one animal from the same colony looked sick. The vet was called in. The animal was isolated and kept separately for one day. The next day the vet came and gave clearance and said it could be returned to the colony.

I spoke to the manager and also the supervisor, and we decided to destroy the animal against the vet's advice. Yet all three of those that were sick looked similar to the one that was destroyed. We called the vet back again. He asked about the last one. We told him that the manager and supervisor decided to destroy it, in case there were some hidden signs we could not see. Unfortunately, these three animals in the same colony did not look well.

The vet asked them to quickly isolate the animals, which we did. He examined the animals and kept silent for a few minutes. He then asked, "How many good animals are there in the colony?"

"There are one hundred seventy of them," I said.

He kept silent and pondered for just over a minute and said, "To save all the animals, not only this group, I advise you to cull the entire colony of the one hundred seventy of them."

He wrote the instructions in the book and then said, "We have to do it, James! We will be doing it in next ten to fifteen minutes. We need to do it to save them all."

This could happen to any animal-breeding facility, but I felt completely helpless, like I had no control over the situation. I was very angry at myself; why did it have to happen now? I hoped it would not build up to be a catastrophe. I told Mary-Ann to go ahead and cull the entire colony.

My eyes swelled, my throat choked up, and my breathing got harder. I quietly told Mary-Ann to get some help or to call Dr. Parker.

Dr. Parker was soon on his way. I was kind of surprised at her summoning Dr. Parker, as if it was a planned event, or knowing Mary-Ann's sensitivity, she must have anticipated my reaction to the news and informed Dr. Parker proactively.

Anyway I asked Mary-Ann, "Did you discuss with my wife about the incident?"

"No," she said. "I have not. But I suspect they will find out sooner or later."

"I will speak to them in a reassuring manner."

Dr. Parker arrived, examined me thoroughly, and said, "As we suspected, a phase of acute anxiety."

He gave me some medication and said, "Take it again before you go to bed. If you still have symptoms by tomorrow morning, please let me know. I will come and check on you again."

As he was about to leave, he suddenly turned, came close to me, and said, "James, remember next week is scheduled for Tijuana. You will be OK if you stay as is."

He left.

CHAPTER 21

MARY-ANN SAVES ME AGAIN

Indeed she did. At least that was what I thought at that time and I was vastly grateful.

After the episode of first culling of one entire colony of the most demanded Sprague Dawley rats, things improved, as we had the environmental-health inspectors, industrial-health inspectors, and our own vet make frequent assessments. Any proposal they came up with, we implemented as advised. So with all the checks and balances, we had very little reason to worry.

Now I was almost to the middle of the third year of my treatment. I continued to feel better after my treatment in Tijuana, yet my risk of catching infection remained very high. Only Mary-Ann and Dr. Parker and other people directly involved with my treatment were allowed in and only with protective gear.

My wife and children were getting increasingly frustrated to just being able to come and see me only a few times a day. They saw that their dad was well, not handicapped, and with no serious symptoms and that he was not apparently suffering with pain or any discomfort, yet he was at a very high risk of getting infection that might lead to death. They understood the risk but felt increasingly dejected at being kept away. But the girls spoke to me on Skype from a few rooms away for hours every day; that kept our morale ticking.

In the next couple of months, even after taking all the possible measures and precautions, a few other colonies got infected and had to be culled. This news traveled fast, and we started to lose our orders and had contracts canceled, which affected our income, which reduced drastically. I was like a prisoner and just could not help.

One day I asked Mary-Ann, "How long do you think this treatment will continue?"

Her answer was, "As long as you benefit from it; it is the best choice we have. Like people who undergo regular dialysis for kidney failure, they continue with renal dialysis regularly until they are able to provide a kidney donor and are physically fit enough to go through the kidney transplant; then they are off dialysis after the transplant. If a donor is not found, then the dialysis continues through their remaining life.

"You have a different situation. We are dealing with a very rare and unusual type of bone-marrow cancer. There is no chemotherapy, surgery, special type of radiotherapy, or any other measure, to our present knowledge, to find out how widespread your cancer is. Unless we know the extent of your bone-marrow cancer, it will be impossible to do a bone-marrow transplant. Eventually we may or will come to that stage when it will be possible, but not at this moment. Again, there is no experience at all on how the bone-marrow transplant will work or react in your case. I am sure the professor has all this in his plans, but being a scientist, he goes by what realistically can be done in your case and moves forward when the time is right. For the time being, to answer your question, we propose to continue your treatment as long as you benefit; if that requires moving you from Boston to Tijuana, that will remain an option.

"Of course, remember that in the beginning you gave the professor your consent. He also gave you a choice to withdraw from the treatment anytime you wish. After that, you may choose to be seen by Dr. Black or anyone you wish, or you may want to be seen by the professor's team; that will also work. In that case, the research foundation will not be able to support you financially for your treatment and compensation for loss of workdays."

"Thanks, Mary-Ann," I said, "for explaining and detailing the relation with the professor and his team that includes you particularly. I know that I am being treated by the best person in the world and receiving the best treatment that is available. It just hurts to see my family sad and so far away, living only three or four doors away. It does, indeed.

"Also, it hurts to see my last thirty-five years of hard work—and with the grace of God, a very successful one—just fizzling away only because of my illness and because of my inattention. So many lives, so many families, will suffer if the business closes down. What will they do?"

The next couple of months were even more critical. Apparently some staff resigned, saying that the future of the company was bleak and they did not want to take any chances.

One day Mary-Ann said, "This is not good for your business. The business still has a huge clientele both in and out of the continent of North America. You have a huge amount of stable assets, which account for a few hundred million. The way it is going now, soon you will be facing bankruptcy. In anticipation of this eventuality, we need to act now and act fast.

"James, I would like you to meet a couple of people soon to discuss matters. I would also like you not to discuss with anyone the possible changes we are anticipating. Life must go on as usual."

Two days later, Mary-Ann came with two men; apparently one of them was a highly respected bankruptcy lawyer from Boston with an international practice, and the other man was from a well-reputed US multinational accounting firm. Mary-Ann had already spent several hours elaborating the current state of my health and the health of my business.

I discussed every detail of my activities, my business affairs, my responsibilities for my family, and so on with the men.

They wanted to find accurate details of my net worth, debts, and receivables and the exact scope of my business. For this, we needed to have a detail discussion with my general manager and the chief accountant.

Mary-Ann would organize the meeting very soon.

"In the meantime," said the lawyer, "to protect you from any lawsuits, we need to establish two trust accounts, one for the business and the other for your family, to tighten all legal protection."

"For the business trust account," said the accountant, "Mary-Ann will be your business partner so that, in your absence, Mary-Ann can operate the account as needed. The second trust account will be for your family. Your wife will be the only operator of the account, and your children will all be members of the family trust, which they may not operate until they become adults and only with the consent of your wife. We will look into the details of the trust's legal standing so that all necessary steps are taken for the smooth running of the trust.

"After the trusts become legal and operational, fifty percent of your reimbursement fee for loss of income for attending the Tijuana facility will be deposited into the family trust. You will receive two checks, one for you and the other for the family trust."

I said, "I have no problem if you deposit one hundred percent to the family trust."

The accountant said that could not be done for legal reasons, especially from the research foundation's point of view, as the payee.

I accepted the proposal, subject to their meeting with my senior administrative staff and the company lawyer and their advice on the proposal.

"That is fine, but to give you immediate legal protection, we need to establish these two trust accounts," said Mary-Ann.

One week later Mary-Ann arranged a meeting with her lawyer and accountant and with our general manager, chief accountant, and legal counsel in a secret place outside our premises. I was present via Skype during the entire meeting, which lasted just over four hours.

My staff had done an exhaustive report, which was sent to me a few days ahead of the meeting.

I was surprised to see our net worth. But the recent performance was poor, still not bad.

We were worth close to $110 million, before assessment of debts and possible severance payment in case we decided to dismantle the operation if no buyer became available in the next six months.

The decision was to seek out potential buyers and make every effort to sell the business while it was still operational and to sell it as a functioning, profit-making business with all the assets with it. It did not take very long. We had three potential buyers, of which the South African company associated with several safari parks looked promising.

Mary-Ann's people and our general manager made a couple of trips to Johannesburg, and the president of the South African company with his team visited Boston and our campus, met our staff, spent a couple of days touring the premises, and went into several animal holdings to meet the caretakers. As it was routine, they were allowed to examine our performance data for a few days. They also met several of our clients in the Boston area, including some of the world-famous medical and biological IT research centers. We all felt that they were reasonably happy, but how deep their happiness was disclosed later to our disappointment.

The president reassured us that this possible purchase proposal would be the top of the agenda of the forthcoming board meeting, which would take place in three weeks' time.

We also had visits from the American companies. They were more deeply investigative about the details of our performance and spent lots of time with senior administrative and curating staff. They looked into the details of the history of the performance of the previous ten years. They met our clients in different institutes within legal boundaries.

In the end, the South African company came with the right offer—$115 million, more or less—as our team agreed to. It was settled. The company would be operationally handed over in six months, while their staff would start working with our staff for a period for acquaintance and introduction to the operation and administration.

According to the agreement, the current staff would have the option to remain in the job with present terms for six months, when they had to deal with a new contract as the incoming owner offered or leave the company with appropriate severance money as agreed with the current employer.

The new company also requested that I stay as member of the board for four years.

In the end, after clearing all the debts, IRS taxes, outstanding bills, and legal and accounting fees, we were left with $63 million, out of which, $5 million was to be deposited in the family trust, and the remaining $58 million would be deposited in our business-trust account.

Nothing could be better.

With her clever action, Mary-Ann saved me again and pulled me out of ruin. Maybe.

CHAPTER 22

MY WIFE AND CHILDREN DRIFT AWAY

As Mary-Ann's involvement in the affairs of my health increased, one day my wife came fully clad in the protective gear, as they had been asked to do to protect me from my family in case I accidentally got infected from my wife or from my children; that would be fatal to me. But my personal life revolved around my family. My wife of twenty-five years, my most darling children, my princesses—what would my life be without them? How were they living without me, being so close but yet so far? That was the saddest, most painful, and most distressing part, and the feeling was like being the living dead. My personal regrets couldn't be expressed in words, no matter how many tears I shed silently. I kept it all to myself without letting it out to my family.

Our emotional ties were eternal. Our psychological expanse was all but one. If one got hurt or was happy, we all felt it. We thought nothing could tear us apart; we would stay as a family forever, come what may.

Just around the end of my third year of treatment, unusually my wife came in to see me with the protective gear on. She asked, "How are you doing? How is the special food being prepared for you? We do our best to keep you from any risk of infection. We wear the clothes they ask us to wear to come to see you. Our visits are getting less and less frequent. This is hurting the children, seeing you so sick, and as your only family, we are helpless to do anything for you, to make you feel better, to sit down with you, and to hold your hands. The children miss being able to hug you. Yet to make Daddy better, they all agreed to do what Mary-Ann says. They want their Daddy back again well and healthy.

"So together we decided to move to another house not far away; it's a bit closer to my work and closer to the schools of all three. We move out this weekend. This way we will keep the doctors and Mary-Ann free from anxiety so that your treatment can continue the best way. We will continue to visit you, as we have been doing and anytime you want us to come."

She was a strong person, very strong indeed, both physically and mentally. She spoke those words deliberately without any hesitation or faltering, yet I could see her eyes getting red, just about to break into tears. The words, instead of coming from the chest, came from the throat, forceful but shallow.

I could feel their pain; I could feel their sadness, frustration, and broken hearts after all.

We were silent for several minutes. I was stunned, heartbroken, and I wanted to get out of my house and on the street to scream, "To hell with my sickness! To hell with the treatment! Why should I live if I am being torn away from my heart, my family, my children, and my life?"

My wife repeated some of the words again. "We want you to get better and be with us forever, yet we must not be hindering your treatment. That is bad for all of us."

This time she broke down and came close to me to hug me.

Someone knocked at the door. She gathered herself, back to her full composure.

I could not keep my composure. I said to my wife, "You don't have to go to another house. That will be devastating to me. How will I live? What is my life worth without you and my princesses?"

She was moving out, but we would not be separated.

That was not true. I couldn't believe what was happening to me.

She again said, "James, we are moving out this weekend. We will pray hard and harder for you. Life must go on. This is the way we see that is best for us. James, you need a nurse. You need someone who can or will protect your money and assets, of which I am no expert nor understand much; you do not need a wife now. Let us be happy with what we have now and be grateful to the heavens for the mercy God has bestowed upon us."

Gradually with a changing tone, changing voice, and changing emotional expression, I felt that she did feel that we must be separated and that this was the best solution.

As my wife left, Mary-Ann entered. "James, are you all right? You look very upset."

"Yes, Mary-Ann! I have never been so much upset before in my life. I am so upset; I do not feel it is worth living a life that you are protecting. My wife just said that she was moving with children to another house as early as the coming weekend. What have I done to myself to deserve this? What have I done to them so that they feel so dejected? It is not my doing that I am sick; I did not want to be sick, to leave my family. What shall I do, Mary-Ann? You tell me. Ask the professor when my treatment will be finished, or will it ever finish? Is there a hope? If there is no hope, what am I doing away from my family? Let me be with them for a few weeks, months, years, or whatever life I have left. Let me go back to them; let them come back to me."

"James, I've heard from your wife before how distressed they are at seeing you suffering alone; they are helpless, just standby watchers. It is the children who miss you the most," she said. "I am sure she misses you no less.

"I am here to look after you the best way one can—as a matter of fact, with the best medical science has to offer at this point in time. You are still alive in spite of the deadly scourge you have; we are all struggling to save you. As we said in the beginning, you are free to stop or suspend our recommended treatment at any time you wish. But we will lose all benefits of being part of this new approach to treatment the professor and his team are engaged with. We lose your free treatment and treatment-related costs, and most important we lose the compensation for the loss of workdays.

"I am indeed very, very sorry for the decision your wife has made. She is indeed a very clever but sensitive person. We chat from time to time about every possible thing that revolves around you, your health, your business, your children, your wife, and your house and household activities. We were even planning to let them go for holidays on us, since they have not been out of this house for nearly three years. It would have done lots of good to their emotional health. I suggested visiting her roots in the West Indies or anywhere they wanted to go to get relief from this claustrophobic, depressing, and hospital-like environment.

"I never got any answer. I assumed that they were not interested. If they feel happy that way, then we must not stop them. The real feeling will emerge after a period of separation. After all, we are all tied to your life, health, and future.

"Now being your business partner, my good senses are telling me to strongly advise you against stopping your treatment, for which we all have worked so hard for nearly the last three years. Your health, your survival, will have a strong impact on the lives of many, including your family, your three little darling daughters, me, and the whole research project the professor has built around your well-being and you being around for a very long time.

"You need not feel guilty about not being able to look after your family. On the contrary, we have made a very wise, generous, and long-lasting arrangement to look after your family's well-being in every respect by creating a trust fund, starting with five million dollars, with the only authorized signatory as your wife at this point, until your daughters become adults, yet they will remain joint signatories as long as your wife wants it that way. We've made sure that they can live a comfortable life without being stressed to earn money for their education and their livelihood throughout their life.

"By the way, the house your wife has chosen to move to will be her own, paid for by the research foundation. At present, she will remain a renter; the rent will be paid from her trust, and the rent will be recycled back to her trust so that it does not cost a penny to your family to live in that house. Even if she wishes to buy the property, funds will come from the trust and again will be recycled back into the trust. That is what the accountant and our lawyers have worked out.

"So, James, you do understand that the foundation is doing everything to keep you happy and able to go on with the program."

I was stunned and overwhelmed!

"Oh! Mary-Ann, you knew well ahead of me that she was going for separation. Perhaps you can also tell me when she will file for divorce?"

"I do not know; what I do know is that I do not know if she will ever file for divorce. We will do everything to dissuade her until we can give you a clean bill of health. A divorce proceeding is not a very pleasant situation to think about now. It might never happen; she might come back to live with you sooner than we think."

All this felt as if the heavens had crashed on me. I had no power to think; I had no power to move. I was dead without being dead.

I had no words to express my gratitude for what Mary-Ann had done, but inside me a voice was telling me to throttle her to death and get out of this prison.

That was what I had to do to send her to hell.

The next morning when Mary-Ann came at my breakfast time, I told her that I needed to go back to my island in order to see my family, whom I had not seen for more than thirty years.

Mary-Ann replied, "I can't give you an answer immediately. I think that will be a good move. But we must discuss with the professor and his team, and if they agree, we must decide when will be the best time."

I was surprised to get such an easy answer. I would wait to hear when I could go to see my people.

CHAPTER 23

DREAM COME TRUE: VISITING MY PEOPLE

A month after I returned to Boston from my session in Tijuana, I asked the professor if I could visit my people in the Caribbean since I had not been back since I had come to the United States just over thirty years ago. Although we had communication through the phone, letters, and recently on Skype, every year one or the other family members' voices were not heard. Gradually it had all stopped seven years ago. I had not heard my parents' voices for the last ten years. No one talked of the missing voices; no one told me about my parents' death. It was so many years since I had spoken to my parents that I had to accept the fact that they had escaped from their mortal bodies and were now in heaven with eternal immortality, peace, and happiness.

As I spoke, I could see that the professor seemed to be agreeing with me about making a visit back home.

"Anyway," he said, "let me discuss with the team, review your case, and weigh all possible risks and unexpected surprising events—those that could adversely affect your heath and even be fatal."

After we returned to Boston, Mary-Ann wanted to speak to me about my trip to the Caribbean.

She said, "The professor and the team said it is a very good idea for your mental health and that of your soul. But you will run a very serious risk of getting a fatal infection, especially in a developing country, considering the resources they might have. That is why they have suggested that both Dr. Parker and I need to travel with you, in case there is any problem from health or travel issues. You will be shielded."

For a minute, I felt choked but thought about all the happiness this would bring. This deep hankering for touching the soil of my land, of my birth, might affect my health and my future in a negative way. I was very deeply hurt that I would not be able to take my wife and children with me. This I would regret forever. Anyway my family had been offered holidays anywhere, including the Caribbean, but they had not taken the offer. It would hurt me more if they rejected my offer. So I sobbed silently, without tears.

I was feeling quite cheerful and looking forward to the trip. We were ready: me, Mary-Ann, and Dr. Parker, my two angelic guardians.

By this time I had become an expert frequent traveler, living in and out of a suitcase. It was summer. Summers in Boston could be chilly with hailstorms, which were not rare. But heat, humidity, and hurricanes were the hallmarks of the Caribbean. We were unprepared mentally and physically to confront the Caribbean fickle weather. But we got in the plane from Boston to Miami anyway and then to the land that I loved. An unbelievably small airport with all the trappings of a big international airport awaited us. There was immigration control, customs, and the revolving carousel perhaps ten or twelve feet across with porters helping to sort your bags and then to carry them through customs. Customs officers were wide awake and seemed to sense the contents of the bag. Generally, people were let go without being stripped to their pants, but when the officers did strip them, they did it to perfection.

One porter was with us all the way from the carousel to the pre-arranged pickup van. In half an hour, we were in the hotel, which had been built on a slave-trading post. *Disgusting*, I thought in the beginning, but the whole design was to honor the suffering of slaves. Some of their fierce, bold leaders were etched on the walls in a magnificent way; instead of feeling sorry for them, I started to feel proud of them, proud of being one of their descendants. Interestingly the entire masterpiece of the black slaves' history was not etched on the wall, to stay forever, by a black man but by a German artist. As far as history goes, the Germans were never big traders of slaves, yet it was a German who captured the emotions and etched them on stone forever.

We all checked into our individual rooms. Mary-Ann said that she wanted to explore this beautiful island on her own for peace. Dr. Parker decided to do the same. I was free to move around.

That was when I decided to go back to my piece of land, where I was born. It was several hundred feet high up in the mountain.

That is where this story began. I found very few people I knew around, very few who recognized me as a baby, as a boy in school, and then into my twenties, feeding chickens, tending cows, goats, pigs, and also the large piece of land my parents had lived off and had wanted me to take over as the eldest son. I had had different ideas. My eyes were on the ships sailing past our coasts and planes flying over our sky. I dreamed of catching one of those and floating away or hanging from one flying past our sky and drifting with them.

Drift I did, but that is at the beginning of the story.

In the evening, we met for dinner. I told them of my real homecoming experience as a drifter, which was what I wanted to do while I was here.

Dr. Parker said, "I sat on the beach and read on the history and people of the region." Like both of us, Dr. Parker, a descendent of a Russian Holocaust survivor of Romanian descent, knew very little about the region. In fact, we admitted that both Mary-Ann and I, who were colored and Caribbean, had much less knowledge about our Caribbean heritage than Dr. Parker had managed to absorb in one and a half days.

Mary-Ann said that while exploring the town on her own, she had discovered that this tiny country had oncology services, including an oncology-treatment center.

Mary-Ann was pleasantly surprised. She was uncertain about the length of James's stay on the island. She pondered that, in case of any emergency, instead of lining up in the local hospital's A-and-E department, of which she has no knowledge at all, and scouting for a knowledgeable and a sympathetic general physician, which might be a challenge, perhaps it would be less of a risk to keep in contact with a professional who would understand James better than any doctor.

On the other hand, she thought that she was neither competent nor privy to the present details of James's condition that wasn't discussed with anyone outside the team of Dr. Parker and those who were working with the professor on the project.

Being torn between the thoughts of James's health and confidentiality of his treatment, she thought to herself that she had some responsibility to bring back James to Boston, at least in a way he came, not in any other form. With the conflict of conscience and courage, her conscience and compassion won. She decided to contact the island's oncologist to keep an eye on James. Dr. Parker's advice and expertise were generally available, but who knew when and how any emergency might crop up, when Dr. Parker might be out of reach.

These were the mixed emotion and logic she was trading in at this point.

She said, "I went to get an appointment for you to see what this oncologist had to say. I went to the office and asked for an appointment and prices for consultation. The nurse or receptionist said that this was a government hospital where all the services were free or practically free to citizens of this country. It was a total surprise to me. I had a short interview with the oncologist who introduced himself as Dr. Arjoon Persaud, and he gave me an appointment for you. He may have some different thoughts. We will go to see him in two days' time. I need a couple of days to gather all the information that he requested.

"Dr. Persaud could be native born, but from what I have found, he has traveled worldwide and seems to have asked all the right questions, like what I would have expected from the professor and his team."

Returning to the hotel, I was very tired from the heat and humidity, which canceled all myths of being in a tropical paradise. But as the sun leaned to the west, a refreshing, cool breeze came past the coconut groves, and with the tropical evergreens high up in the hills, it pacified the frustration of the day. I must say that it had something to do with the Californian climate, which had completely corrupted my pleasure sensations and made me intolerant to any other weather outside of California. Boston was physically intolerable but mentally so engaging that physical discomfort was all washed away by intellectual high winds. This was long before we had to deal with one of the world's rarest, most misdiagnosed, and most poorly understood illnesses that affected few human beings but excited several minds trying to know the unknown and perhaps find a cure.

In the last three days, the tropical thrill of nature had been slowly enchanting me. Both Mary-Ann and I reminisced about a lot of our childhood in this haven, which we had left for the lure of a better life. How a life can be better than this?

I collected all the information I could get for Dr. Persaud, and we went to see him in the local hospital. The staff had already checked my nationality's authenticity and identified me as a national, since public services and health care are free or heavily subsidized for all nationals.

He greeted us and asked us to sit down while he went through the documents I had submitted.

"One question," asked Dr. Persaud. "Do you know that you have a cancer of the bone marrow, a very rare cancer indeed? But I do not see exactly what treatment you have had for the last three years. I did not see a report of your bone marrow examination, since we know that your cancer started in the bone marrow."

I knew that I had had several bone-marrow examinations, especially for the research. I was kind of surprised that not a single report was included, particularly about the treatment. It appeared to have been deliberately excluded. I immediately sent a message to the professor, and within ten minutes, we received several bone-marrow-examination reports.

Dr. Persaud went through the documents and commented that, in some of the marrow, it appeared that the disease was very aggressive and in others not so, even appearing to be almost like normal bone marrow. He specifically wanted to know the treatment I had undergone so far.

I said, "I have had periodical plasmapheresis but could not get any more information from the documents I had."

Dr. Persaud took me to another examination room, and Mary-Ann was allowed to be present while I was being examined. A very thorough examination, indeed, was conducted. He had many questions about what I had reported and many more we were unable to answer.

He said, "It is a difficult disease to treat, especially in the Caribbean. We see many more in this region, compared to what we see in the continent of North America. Once treated, a majority of them do well for years, eventually dying from the uncontrollable disease or serious side effects from long-term use of cancer medicine. But they do have several years of fruitful and enjoyable life.

"Your illness is not a typical one, and most of the atypical cases like you do not do well with the treatments currently available for typical cases. On the other hand, some atypical cases like yours do well. With the available knowledge and technology, we only can try, expecting to fail but hoping otherwise. Even to fail, one has to try. One can't fail if one does not try, but not failing in this case is not winning. My best senses say to treat you as if you were diagnosed yesterday, last week, or last month, not three years ago. I will give you a plan of treatment. I suggest strongly that you give yourself an opportunity even to fail, but I will look forward to success."

So Dr. Persaud gave an overall plan of medication, lifestyle, diet, and so on. Dr. Persaud told me that if I started the treatment, I should be seen and monitored by another oncologist who had the experience of managing these diseases.

Mary-Ann and I both seemed to be in favor of the suggestion made by the "village oncologist" and his approach to treating me. We took note of everything that was said or written.

Since I was indeed feeling so much better after seeing the doctor and my own birthplace, old school pals, and some distant cousins who were all so welcoming and loving, I thought I could come back to live here for the rest of my life. In Boston and in America, there was lots of life but only trickles of soul. Boston had given me my life and my family, but at the same time, Boston had torn away my family from my heart. I was still licking the wounds of separation from my wife and children.

So we spent a couple of weeks more in the tropical heaven. Slowly but surely Mary-Ann was engulfing me with her love and affection and her apparent deep concern for my health. We had a happy and enjoyable time in the paradise, and then came the call of duties, call of schedules, call for tests, and most importantly a call from Dr. Parker to instruct us to return to Boston for the tests to prepare for the trip to Tijuana.

So we left and returned to the same routine, same precautions, same isolation, and same tests by Dr. Parker, which were followed by trips to Tijuana.

My contact with my family and children was becoming rare; sometimes I had to force them to bring my family "home." My medical team and support were not happy when this happened. But I always had the option of quitting the project and plunging into the unknown. I would die, and at the same time, the professor's project would have the same destiny. This was a symbiotic existence with both gaining. No one loses, or both lose. No winners but both satisfied.

This went on for another year. During this time, I felt that I was getting weaker and weaker, even losing my balance on occasions. I was very thirsty. I had the feeling that we must have come to the end of the rope; we couldn't move any further. This must be the end. Was this how it felt? Was this what the end looked like? Then during my earlier visits to Tijuana, I asked the professor about the treatment plan that Dr. Persaud from the remote Caribbean place had suggested. The professor looked at the papers I had from my hometown oncologist.

He looked intently at the papers and said, "Very good advice for people who have bone-marrow cancer like yours but not exactly like yours; that is where we are stuck. We could have followed these instructions three years ago, but the chance that we would have lost was more than eighty percent. What we have done with the new way has given you a nearly healthy life. You have security and protection, not only of your health but also of your assets and your family. These are side issues that may not be important for you. You have worked hard for thirty or more years to gain the material status that you have achieved; it would be a mere pipe dream for many of us, but your spirit, which led you to take part in the research, is what matters to us the most. We have learned from you more than what we were able to provide you with. We admire your courage and admiration for truth seekers. That is what matters the most to me and to the entire group of people who are taking care of you. Some of them you see frequently, but the others, the scientists working behind the closed doors day in, day out are all grateful. We have come a long way so far.

"However, as we said in the beginning, you are free to decide to stop our management and start any treatment that you might choose; we will give you all support you need from us. Unfortunately, the foundation's financial commitment will cease."

The life of a prisoner, like what I had now, was intolerable. My heart cried for my family, my children, my company, managers, workers, fresh air, a walk in Fennel Park by the river, strolling on

Copley Square by the bay front, and most importantly the spirit of Boston, which made me what I was—or what I had been. I pined to return once again to my native land. It was almost a year since I had visited.

After meeting Dr. Persaud there, I had been reassured that someone would take care of me if I got really sick.

After I returned from Tijuana and the discussion with the professor and him being so clear and generous to me, I told Mary-Ann that I would continue with the treatment as the professor suggested, considering the excellent physical and financial support I was receiving. But I would like to visit my native land again, see my people, breathe the air, drink the water, and mess with the dust in which I was born, played, and grew up from being a baby to a toddler to a big man.

Mary-Ann listened to my babbling, my incoherence, perhaps the result of, or maybe the reaction to, the separation from my family. I missed them so dearly, so deeply, that I would not be surprised if I was confused and making incorrect decisions all around.

Mary-Ann looked at me, kept quiet for a couple of minutes, and said, "Why not? We had a great time a year ago. I will ask the professor and let you know soon when we can make the arrangements, if at all."

I found that Mary-Ann was more enthusiastic about looking after me and my affairs than before.

My world revolved around Mary-Ann and Dr. Parker, sometimes the physiotherapist and nutritionist, and the psychologist on rare occasions. Sometimes weeks would go by before I saw my family: my wife and my children. I had a total disregard and revulsion for TV or any electronic amusement. I did read lots of books, more in last three years than what I had done in the last fifty years. That was the bonus for it all.

CHAPTER 24

THE LAST VOYAGE

I was very happy and cheerful and looking forward to the trip to my native land. Dr. Parker did all the preparations from a medical point of view, while Mary-Ann handled the travel arrangements in such a way that we would be back before the next scheduled visit to Tijuana.

Dr. Parker said, "James, you are looking better, happy, and energetic, but your test results are not that happy. You are not far from requiring another apheresis or maybe more."

We were planning to be away for three weeks, which might have to be cut short. If it had to be, it had to be.

"Now that both of you have made all the arrangements, let us stick to our plan. But if Dr. Parker thinks that the risks are high enough for us to cancel the journey, then let us do so," I said.

Mary-Ann was hesitant to accept. She said, "If we are really in trouble, then we will shift by an air ambulance. He does not have many issues; let us have the trip, and we will be vigilant anyway."

"Let us have another discussion with the new test results," said Dr. Parker.

"I thought we had already presented them to the professor and the team," said Mary-Ann.

"Yes," said Dr. Parker. "Still, I would like to speak to him once before we take off."

"Fine, let us do that then," she said.

In ten minutes, the professor was on the line. He asked me some questions about my energy and general health. Then the three of them discussed for another ten to fifteen minutes.

Dr. Parker came to me and said, "We all agreed that the risk is there, but we will go along with the planned trip."

I thought to myself, *If I am taking a trip on a flight with hundreds of unknown people, who knows who might be carrying what infection that will jump on me and may cause havoc. But in fact I am no threat simply because I am so well protected and covered by antibiotic armor that I can hardly be harboring infectious germs.* So I said, "I must see my wife and children in their new home and find out how they are doing. I have not seen them for weeks."

Both Mary-Ann and Dr. Parker agreed, and we made a trip to my family's new home.

It was five o'clock in the evening. Both my wife and children had returned home after work and school and had time to change and rest a bit.

They were very surprised to see me outside my room unprotected, not even a mask to check my breathing.

"Surprised?" I said. "I am cured, so I do not need any protection anymore. No one is of any threat to me, nor am I to anyone."

The children screamed, "Daddy! Daddy! You are better; you must come and stay in this house, or we should all go back to our own house."

My wife had a look of happiness, but the expression was also telling me that it might not happen until I was cleared of all infection and, in her words, "human infestation." What she meant was, until Mary-Ann's overwhelming influence on our family and overpowering command on us was all completely cleaned away, the possibility of us living together was even farther from remote.

Mary-Ann said, "Since we are going to visit his native land again, there is no risk or harm visiting his family right in Boston."

The children screamed again, "I want to come with you, Daddy," all at the same time again and again.

When the excitement slowed down, Mary-Ann cautiously said, "Your daddy is not completely better yet. But he wanted to visit his birthplace again, so we thought it would be a good idea to let him do that. I am sure the next time when we plan another trip, you all will be welcome to join us."

"Oh, nice," said all three, with no word from my wife.

Mary-Ann said, "We are planning to visit for three weeks, but we may return sooner. We will let you know about his activities on this voyage and any change in our plan because of his health. Let us get ready, and we will be seeing you soon."

So the next day, we boarded the plane for my beloved homeland. Five hours of a long haul and one more hour of a short jump trip, and then we were in the land of my birth and that of my forefathers. I couldn't remember how many of us had catapulted ourselves across the sea, across the ocean, above and beyond the mountain. One for sure was my uncle who had given me the life I had back in Boston.

They said that many more souls of this land lived off the land than on the land itself. Many of my compatriot islanders lived not only in Boston but also across the entire continent of North America and in other parts of the world.

Why did I leave? Why did anybody leave this God-given land of paradise? Its deep-green color looked unbelievably exotic, with colorful flowers and an abundance of fruits lying on the ground for nature to consume and that, away from the ground, graced the dinner tables of lords, ladies, stars and starlets, and famous and infamous. One could hardly escape the lust for fruits, flowers, and fauna of this land.

It seemed that, like many others, I had discovered my birthplace again, which I had lost for several decades. It had come alive to me again.

In our hotel, we took a long rest, overdue and well deserved.

The next day Mary-Ann said, "James, as we discussed, we should see Dr. Persaud just for a chat and any new advice he can give us. It is also a very good idea to get yourself checked, since you were not too well when we left Boston. Everyone was concerned, but for your mental well-being, we all agreed to let you take the chance to visit your home, people, friends, relatives, and also the environment that you grew up in."

Dr. Persaud was very prompt and started to ask about all that happened to me, from my illness, treatment, general health, my family, and my business. I knew these questions since I had spoken to many doctors, sort-of doctors, and wannabe doctors, so the answers came spontaneously and sometimes came through a heavenly voice.

I said, "Nothing new has happened. I went regularly to have my blood cleaned, sometimes in four weeks and other times in two weeks. I do feel better after each cleaning. But I feel that my energy is not as great and is gradually getting less and less after each cleaning. My zest for life and living is dampened more frequently; the feeling lasts longer, and escaping from this state also takes longer. I have become forgetful, which is unlike me; this is also making me more nervous about my future. I do not have any pain, but I do have a throbbing headache from time to time. My bowels are constipated, and my urine seems to be heavy."

He listened and made notes as we continued to discuss and respond to his questions.

Then he asked Mary-Ann about the test results from Tijuana. Mary-Ann had some that she gave to him. He carefully scanned all the results.

Then he said, "James, you came to see me one year ago, and I prescribed to you a course of chemotherapy. There is huge amount of data suggesting that you could have responded to the standard treatment; although the chances are not that high, it is not zero. Did you go through the course?

"James, we can only fail if we try; if we do not try, then we will never fail and will never know if we will fail or succeed. All I see is that he had frequent plasmapheresis. In my opinion, it was too frequent. I am sure that the professor knows better than a country doc. But from what I can see, your condition has progressively gotten worse, but the speed of deterioration may have been lessened by what is being done in Tijuana."

Mary-Ann said, "The standard treatment may have been included in the complex treatment regimen offered to him in Tijuana." But she did not have the exact answer.

"What I understand," said the doctor, "is that you are planning to stay here for a few months; then I suggest that we start him on the standard treatment and keep him well enough so that he can return to Boston in one piece."

Mary-Ann felt somehow reassured, but she did not want to fully start me on any form of drastic regimen without discussing with the professor or one of his team members.

She did discuss it with the professor and his team, but the response was to hold off. By that time it was much past midnight, and she was planning to talk with the doctor early morning the next day.

But just after midnight, as I was trying to get up to go to the washroom, I suddenly felt severe back pain and went back to bed, hoping it would wear off. When I woke up again, I found that I had lost complete strength in both legs and was unable to move. The sensation gradually got worse. Now I no longer had the urge to pass urine any more. I called out to Mary-Ann.

Mary-Ann woke up and was surprised to see what had happened. She stared at me in horror, but she had a plan to handle the situation. She immediately called the professor. His response was to immediately move me out and bring me to Tijuana, after the local doctor had seen me.

The suggestion was to move me in an air ambulance, which was difficult to obtain at that time. For me to return on the scheduled flight would take time. So I was admitted to the local hospital.

The doctor found me paralyzed from the waist down; my bladder was full and distended.

The next morning my backache got much worse, and no painkiller was good enough. The doctor carried out several tests, and to his horror, he found that there was not a single bone in my body that was not involved with my cancers. Some areas showed that the bones were at serious risk of fracture. My blood was thick, almost like jelly, due to too much protein, the doctor thought. I was complaining of severe pain, unable to move; my speech was slurred, and I was confused.

The doctor said, "With this condition, he is not able to fly."

If Mary-Ann wanted to take me out of the hospital, then someone responsible had to take me out against medical advice and sign the required medico legal documents.

The doctor expressed to Mary-Ann that it was much easier to fly a dead body, when medico legal requirements were less stringent, than to fly a seriously ill person who died on board, where the medico legal process was much more complex and overridingly cumbersome.

Then the doctor asked Mary-Ann what her relationship with me was.

She answered, "I am his business partner."

Then the doctor asked, "Are you legally authorized to be responsible or authorized to make decisions that are legally binding out of the realm of his business arrangements?"

Mary-Ann was rather upset at the audacity of the country doctor for questioning her about the legality of her making any decision on my behalf.

The doctor said, "Mary-Ann, my main aim is to make him comfortable with whatever means we can use to meet my objective. There is a request for a lot of medications for treatment, which are urgently needed. I hope you will be able to assist us in procuring the medications. All those prescribed are available in the hospital pharmacy. All we are missing is funds to purchase those. We do not know anyone else whom we can inform, other than you."

"I will do my best, Doctor!" she said.

The next day the doctor waited for the medicine. Mary-Ann was not to be seen anywhere; her phone was also dead.

The doctor somehow managed to obtain most of the medications and continued with treatment.

In the meantime, I fractured my right arm and needed internal metal support to fix it, which was not available due to the lack of cash. My pain and discomfort were agonizing and increasing as time passed. The little hospital did what it could with the modest resources they had available. Sadly the business partner had vanished when she was needed most.

At this point I was absolutely bedridden and completely unfit for any form of transfer except in an air ambulance with a full intensive-care-unit support.

CHAPTER 25

THE EMISSARY APPEARS

The following day Mary-Ann was seen with another man.

Mary-Ann was missed very much, she was told. She replied that she had had some very important personal business to attend to. She had had to return to Boston immediately and had to leave suddenly but had no time to contact anyone. She apologized for her "irresponsible" behavior.

The man came with her and introduced himself as the chief public-relations officer of the San Diego–based International Agency for Research on Human Rare Diseases, a subsidiary of the parent organization, "the research foundation." He called himself Spencer and was a lawyer by profession.

He said that the foundation had been paying for my treatment for the last four years and would continue to support my treatment cost, whatever was needed.

Then Spencer said to the doctor, "Perhaps you would like to give him treatment for his bone-marrow cancer, whatever you think is best. We will get anything you want. All we are hoping is that you will make him well and stable enough so that we can take him back to Boston to his family so that they can be together for whatever life he has left. It would be even better if you with your expertise can give him another new lease on life. All of us around him will be enormously grateful."

The doctor said, "Mr. Spencer, it is not too late to start his actual treatment for his bone-marrow cancer, which was diagnosed four years ago. He was under your watch all these years, and what did you do for him?"

"My apologies, Doctor," said Mr. Spencer. "He was under the care of the best-known specialist internationally. The treatment and management plan the specialist developed must have contributed to give him at least four years of life. James has one of the most rare and difficult bone-marrow cancers to treat."

The doctor kept silent for a few moments and then said, "It must be a very difficult condition to treat but thanks anyway for all the moral and physical support we have received. I will think seriously about starting his recommended treatment for bone-marrow cancer, if he is in a reasonable shape to tolerate the treatment, which has many side effects."

A third man joined in, trying to rescue me. He introduced himself to Dr. Persaud, the oncologist, as Dr. Parker from Boston, who had been involved in my treatment from the very beginning. He wanted to help in any way he could to make me well enough to fly home to Boston, back to my family.

The doctor said, "Let us get to work and try our best to do just that. But I am afraid it may be too late to offer any real help for a meaningful life."

Dr. Parker said to Dr. Persaud, "We understand the situation, but our help and our prayers are with you. Anything you can do for this man, anything at all, will be appreciated."

Then the doctor went to the ward to decide where to begin.

I was in so much pain and discomfort that I was partly delirious and short of breath. The doctor examined me. With the new medications, there were some improvements, but I was still delirious.

I was constantly saying, "My princesses, I can't go without seeing you. My three little gems, I miss you so much; I love you so, so much."

The doctor had no idea about what "gems" I kept babbling about.

I was kept going for a few more days. The request from my Boston team was, "Please do what you can so that we can take him back to his family."

The doctor could not perform a plasmapheresis, but he requested dialysis.

He was politely told, "Why dialyze a dying man?"

He replied, "He would not have been a dying man had we allowed the dialysis procedure for him earlier."

"He is a dying man, nonetheless; why dialyze?"

The struggle went on for a few more days. I was lucid and alert. I showed Mary-Ann a letter I was asked by Mr. Spencer to sign. I asked her to read it and advise me.

The letter came from the chairman of the California foundation taking care of my treatment. I was being asked to sign a letter saying that I relinquished any claim on any materials, tissue, or body fluid from me that had been used for the purpose of research or tests and on the results, which might lead to the discovery of any marketable product in any shape and form.

The doctor was confused. Why was I being asked to relinquish any claim on my results? He could not understand.

Later in the doctor's office, Mr. Spencer was waiting. After formal reintroduction, he gave an impression of calm and stability and requested that the doctor convince me to sign the letter, even from his sick bay. Dr. Persaud had to discuss the request further with James to understand the relations better before he could take any action.

The doctor was still trying to understand, but he told Mr. Spencer that under no circumstances would he instruct any patient of his to sign a legal document while he was admitted in a hospital bed. That was final.

The doctor said, "Aside from the weight of moral authority, the document will have little value with James's consent without a legal attestation. The legal counsel will need the state of his mental competence under the circumstances, even if he is physically well enough to agree to your proposal. In this instance, a psychiatrist's consultation has to come from me, the treating physician, and I do not see any sign of that coming anytime soon."

Mr. Spencer said, "I entirely agree with you, sir, and respect your decision. We will wait and help you with any medication or any other support you need to pull James out of this crisis."

The doctor was reassured and said, "Let us fight together and hope for the best. Keep in touch; I will keep you informed about his progress."

The doctor continued with what he could do. I was still in severe pain, requiring high doses of morphine. I was also frequently delirious.

The doctor kept pleading for dialysis and for him to be allowed to fix my broken and twisted right arm.

A couple of days later, Mr. Spencer came for an update at the doctor's office. He looked around and spoke to some of the staff.

"Mr. Spencer is a charming man, gentle and polite," one of the nurses commented. As he entered the doctor's office, after exchanging greetings, he started to speak.

"How amazing it is to see such a wonderful, well-organized, disciplined, and clean setup you have here in one of the most remote corners in the developing world. We in the developed world could not have imagined the existence of such a facility in these places."

Mr. Spencer said that he was impressed indeed. He and the foundation could help to make the doctor's center better, and should he require any equipment or logistic support, the foundation would be ready to support him. Mr. Spencer also said that the foundation offered grants for research and also to travel to attend scientific and health-related conferences. These grants were not restricted to any nation or nationality but were granted by merit and encouraged applicants from outside the United States and Canada.

"Thank you, Mr. Spencer," the doctor said. "That is very encouraging indeed. As you see, we have enough scope to expand both clinically and logistically. I will prepare a comprehensive proposal and contact you as soon as I am ready."

Then Mr. Spencer said, "I came to get an update on James. How is he doing? As a layperson, I did not see much change. Do you think he is well enough to go through the processes of giving us the consent and signing the letter?"

It was still about signing that letter.

The doctor said, "He is not well enough to even speak; he is delirious most of the time, calling for his family and his children while in delirium. He is in no shape to go anywhere."

"You see!" said Mr. Spencer. "That is why we all want to take him back to his family, while he is still breathing."

"I agree," said the doctor. "But not soon."

Mr. Spencer left.

The doctor came back to the ward to check on me again. As he came closer to my bed, he called my name. "James! James!" But I did not pay him any attention.

The doctor was surprised to see me holding my iPhone with my broken, twisted arm stretched out. The doctor was surprised that I could stretch my arm unsupported without seemingly any pain.

I was speaking loudly. "My darlings, my darlings, I love you all so much. I miss you all so much; my heart is aching forever to hold you close to my chest. My angels, please come to me; please come to me."

The phone fell from my hand to my chest. The doctor could see on the screen that there were three young women crying and saying, "Dad! Dad! Please talk to us. Dad, we can't see you anymore. Dad, please speak. Dad, please speak. Dad, please do not leave us alone. Look, Mum is right here behind us. Dad! Dad! Please speak, Dad; *please* speak, *please* speak."

The screen went blank.

It was absolute silence as a numbing sensation fell on the doctor, darkness around him. As a doctor and an oncologist witnessing the "end of life" is not uncommon. Yet he had doubted what he was seeing. The faces of little girls on the cell-phone screen were too vivid and their plea to James to speak was too crushing. Dr. Persaud wished not to believe the total stillness that had befallen James. He also wished James to speak, scream, or ask for help. The doctor checked James. He was pulseless. He was not breathing, and his eyes did not respond. His head was tilted to one side. James was cured forever. He could go anywhere.

"I am not stopping you James and even if I tried, I am incapacitated. You are free to go anywhere you want to go. You are really free," said the doctor to himself. "My only regret," mumbled the doctor, "is that I had no chance to help you, James." The doctor's vision got blurred as he left.

Neither Mary-Ann nor Mr. Spencer nor Dr. Parker was to be found anywhere. Apparently they had all checked out from their hotel early that morning.

The doctor contacted the local parish on the island where James had been born. They took the body and buried him in the same cemetery where most likely his mother was buried.

CHAPTER 26

MARY-ANN'S CONFESSION

About a month after James died, the incident was still very much alive in doctor's mind. He remained totally puzzled about the whole affair. Who was James? Who were these people? Why had they suddenly disappeared? What about Spencer's promises to help him and the clinic? Dr. Persaud could not contact the professor or his team or even James's family. It all seemed to have disappeared into thin air. Doctor still had regrets that he had been unable to do the minimum to help James. A self-made, black multimillionaire who had no money to purchase additional equipment needed for his treatment that the government hospital could not provide had died a dejected pauper.

Mary-Ann appeared in smart attire and walked in a spritely manner as she entered the consulting room. She was as pretty as ever and clear, eloquent, and precise as she spoke. She apologized in a sincere tone for not being in touch and for her sudden disappearance.

"All of these things were beyond my control," she said. "I returned here just to speak to you. I have no real connection to this country, no friends, no relatives, no associates, except for James and then yourself. This place was certainly a gift from God, close to the heavens. That is the best memory that I have.

"But I have come here to tell you the worst of my memory. Do I have to tell you all this? Of course not. But having seen you in the last days with James, I felt deeply that you ought to know the world we live in, the world that shapes us and who I am, Mary-Ann, whom you have seen so close to James.

"I hail from Grenada, but I spent all my formative years and adult life in the United States. I am very lucky to have an active academic brain, so I got firsts and medals in almost any test I took. Eventually I ended up in UCLA and Berkley for a period of time and became a graduate student of Professor Frank Hooper at UCSD, and within the shortest time allowed, I graduated with a PhD in biochemical genetics. My life changed when I became an intellectual partner of the professor and he became my mentor.

"He is an astute thinker and a prolific writer and speaker. He is a clinical hematologist and oncologist by training, but his main interest is bone-marrow disorders, especially that of cancer. He has had profound international impact on observations of disease processes of various marrow disorders and still commands respect as a pioneering thinker. His brilliance attracted me, and I am still reeling from it. The professor asked me questions, which I answered to the best of my ability. He responded, 'I believe all your answers are correct until any of them are proved wrong.' Nothing can be more morally and intellectually uplifting than the comments made by the professor about my reply to his questions.

"I was happy working with his cases and labs, researching, producing, and publishing. I presented in the international congresses, meeting people of different countries, different languages, different cultures, different ideas, and different ways of interpretation, which made me even more world-wise and less book- and publication-wise. In one of these meetings, I met Mr. Spencer, who introduced himself as a professor of biochemistry in the Swiss Academy of Science in Bern. We met several times after and started to discuss marketing of potential promising drugs. That was an interesting route for me.

"Then one day he introduced me to a Ukrainian scientist, and the discussion was to get relevant information about the drug so that we could reproduce it in our lab. I needed to study the intellectual-property laws of the European Union and also that of Ukraine. I went to Kiev, the capital of Ukraine, and scouted for the owner and found him. I introduced myself and had several dinners and nights out. Eventually he trusted me to discuss his research project. He was impressed with my interpretation, and within weeks, I had all the documents we needed to recreate the medication in a lab in Switzerland. Within months, it went through the European Commission's drug-approval body and was in the market for use.

"I got several calls and e-mails from the gentleman in Kiev, but I never responded. Mr. Spencer was highly impressed with the smooth running of my operation. I was rewarded handsomely. I mean, real handsomely.

"One evening while I was in Boston, I got a call from my friend in Kiev. I was surprised. He said he just happened to be in Boston for a conference and some negotiations and that perhaps I would like to join him for the dinner and the meeting, since my ability to grasp the essence of any situation is quick and to the point. He complimented my ability to communicate appropriately in differing situations.

"I said, 'Let me check my schedule, and I will call you back in a few minutes.'

"I called Mr. Spencer and let him know about the dinner and the meeting invitation. He said to keep it and to go there at least ten or fifteen minutes early.

"I did as he said. The man from Kiev was there on the dot. As he got out of his limousine, three big men surrounded him, and he followed them to another car.

"I immediately got a call from Mr. Spencer, who asked me if I would like a dinner partner since he was ready and waiting. He said, 'Unfortunately, the gentleman from Kiev will not come and will never invite you for another dinner.'

"Having witnessed Mr. Spencer's action, I started to understand the essence of Mr. Spencer's modus operandi. I felt a sense of loyalty and commitment in Mr. Spencer's behavior and felt he might be trustworthy in business sense and also for my personal protection.

"Then I took a couple of more similar assignments in Russia. Each time I had a different name and a different look. The first one was a private-jetliner owner, a black beauty jetting around the world with Mr. P., one of the wealthiest men in Russia. He was mad about me, fell in love, and eventually was willing to sell his company to his rival and go away to spend the rest of his life somewhere in the Caribbean, on his own island. The transfer was done all legally, but the one billon due to him never came. He committed suicide.

"I was paid in millions. I needed no job to support me anymore, and Mr. Spencer was ecstatic. My confidence became stronger and stronger in discharging these espionage missions and completing the missions successfully. In that way, I accumulated millions and spent millions.

"I was a scholar, and I never knew I had any other talent beyond the books, securing grades in examination, lab experiments, and preparation for presenting and publishing research results. My talent for deciphering minds, bank accounts of rich and famous, and breaking the thoughts of intellectuals are very new, and I am told I am just as good in these activities as in securing the highest grade in any academic competition. I could not have felt better, before these feelings were instilled in me. I realized this talent was entirely dependent on my looks that God had given to me.

"One of the most daring missions I had was to be friendly with an Eastern European arms dealer who supplied arms to anyone ready to pay him the right amount of money. I got friendly with him and gradually learned about his dealings, routes, and specifics of arms dealing. Then I informed Mr. Spencer. For several months, the man's planes were unable to deliver the goods to the right places and instead went to the hands of the government or his rivals.

"Once Mr. Spencer's private jet came for me, and I was asked to meet him in a secluded place in Mongolia. An hour after we took off from Uzbekistan, I heard my private cabin door suddenly being opened; a hostess appeared with a tray in one hand and a gun in the other, aimed at me. I was startled. All I could ask was, why? Before she could raise her arm to fire, she collapsed, and the gun was never shot, while the champagne glass shattered into pieces.

"Another hostess quickly changed into my assailant's clothing and asked me to keep quiet and to pretend that I had been shot dead. The body was swiftly removed. Suddenly the screen lit up, and there was my Bulgarian boyfriend.

"He said, 'Sorry, Mary-Ann, I trusted you, and you diverted my luck. That is never going to happen again. I will meet you in Ulaanbaatar.'

"Within hours, the plane landed in Ulaanbaatar. As my friend got on the plane, the plane took off again. Two young ladies came, disarmed him, and completely stripped him naked. One voice said, 'Mary-Ann, wake up, and see your boyfriend for the last time.' He was surprised to see me alive and unhurt.

"'Mary-Ann, you are well and unhurt. Please come to me and give me my clothes. Who are these people doing this to us?'

"An American voice on the TV answered. Mr. Spencer said from the screen, 'Sir, please look at Mary-Ann for the last time. You plotted to take her life, and now I will take yours.'

"The floor opened up, and he fell through the door to a lower chamber. The floor door closed again, and I could hear as if the wheels were opening up. In fact, from the lower chamber, the Bulgarian was dropped from the jet, somewhere in the middle of the Gobi Desert. Our plane was directed back to fly to Astana, where Mr. Spencer was waiting.

"He asked, 'How do you feel? That should have never have happened. We monitored his every movement and knew well ahead of time his plans and actions.'

"Later I got friendly with a Greek shipping tycoon. He fell in love with me, created a billion-dollar trust for me, and wanted to marry me. The marriage never happened, but the trust came with me and Mr. Spencer and his associates. I got my millions for a job well done.

"The same fate happened to an Egyptian business magnate. He was put in federal prison for drug-and-arms-smuggling charges, but his entire estate was dismantled and divided between Mr. Spencer's partners. I was similarly paid handsomely.

"About four years ago, when Professor Hooper was consulted concerning James's illness I got involved as the professor's emissary to look after James. Not just his health but also the overall socioeconomic aspect. The professor was happy to accept James for treatment. One of the professor's major interests is to understand the nature of James's bone-marrow cancer. He tried to study all the cells in the bone marrow. He studied their individual protein-production capability and the nature of altered proteins from the affected cells. Sometimes the proteins were very high, and at other times, the count was infinitely low.

"His hypothesis was to study the low or negligible protein-producing genes affected by the illness and to possibly determine how one could restore or reverse the disease process if one could structurally repair the genes and have them produce normal amounts of proteins. He had an excellent team of genetic engineers who were even able to identify the genes. They repaired them and made them replicate, but his team of scientists were unable to produce the proteins that their normal counterparts could.

"Then he tried to collect the deficient proteins from a healthy individual, but it was not effective, even if the deficiency was corrected. Culturing the disease-causing cells from both healthy and diseased individuals was also ineffective.

"So in desperation, his attention was focused on the remaining fluid after all the proteins were removed except the ones that were significantly reduced or immeasurable. That means this fluid only contained a very minute quantity of proteins produced by damaged cells or affected cells. Even from a small quantity of molecules, a large amount of proteins can be synthesized. That is his current research.

"His research team advised to try treating patients with James's condition with the supernatants only, which might contain few molecules but might be effective. If we collected enough plasma, then the numbers might be enough to achieve some benefit.

"So the question was to scout and recruit patients from all over the world.

"Here Mr. Spencer's international connections became very useful. With the partnership of Dr. Parker, they were able to identify three patients of the same disease who were willing to try the treatment: one sheikh from the Middle East, another businessman from Brunei, and the third one from South Africa in the diamond business. They were all given the last word from their doctors and several internationally reputed centers. They had no end of cash, but their lives were running too short for their wealth to be any value for much longer.

"Dr. Parker and Mr. Spencer visited each patient as emissaries of the research project and emphatically explained the innocuous side effects; yet the chance of gaining life was fifty-fifty. It was much better than zero-zero, as per their specialists. Huge financial arrangements were worked out in hundreds of millions per treatment to be given every two to four months, depending on their condition between the patients and Mr. Spencer's company. Now Dr. Parker and Mr. Spencer, with their tentacles, had managed to find three more patients: one in Europe, one in Central Asia, and one in the South Pacific islands.

"The professor's treatment plan had been that after James's plasma had been cleaned of protein molecules that are in abundance, it would be cleaned again to separate protein molecules that are present in minute quantity that are usually present in abundance in healthy persons. These are supposed to have been produced by suppressed genes owing to James's illness. After several collections enough proteins may be collected for treatment of patients who are suffering from same disease as James.

"So for the advantage of all the other patients, it was decided that James would have regular plasma cleaning and be given all supporting treatments. Since his blood was so thick with proteins, he had to go through the blood cleansing every two to three weeks.

"He did not receive any chemotherapy, since chemotherapy is likely to kill James's bone-marrow cancer cells and by doing so will reduce the amount of proteins needed for harvesting, which are used for treatment of other patients. James was also on a trial to observe the role of plasmapheresis alone.

"He never got any actual treatment that might have helped him. On the contrary, ways and means were adopted to increase the protein production by controlled aggravation of his bone-marrow cancer. His plasma effluent has been sold for hundreds of millions for treatment and research. Bone-marrow samples were being sold for research for hundreds of millions. The main buyers were Japanese and Russians.

"Mr. Spencer, Dr. Parker, and their associate established this 'research foundation' for research and treatment for rare cancers. The foundation is supporting close to a billion US dollars for medical research. The source of its funds is not clear, but certainly treating superrich patients with materials extracted from James's plasma has a significant part to play to generate revenue for the foundation of this magnitude. So the support they offered to James from patients and research institutes was minute compared to what the foundation was making. The professor was awarded funding for his original research by the foundation. He had no idea about the source of funds generated by the foundation, neither the actual financial incentive James was receiving from the foundation. I was the intermediary, who kept the professor completely in the dark on the financial management and, at the same time, kept James compliant to the regimen offered by the professor's team. So it was the most important job to keep

James ready for treatment at any cost, even if that meant breaking his family apart. That is what we had to do to keep James alive for this scheme. He was never allowed to have any kind of standard treatment of his bone-marrow cancer. Again, to maintain his compliance, we had to sell off his business.

"Also a few other animal breeders for research were friends of Mr. Spencer and Dr. Parker. Spencer and his group created better business opportunities for their friends and relatives.

"It was an absolute necessity to keep James alive at any cost in order to run the foundation. James alive with disease was more desired than James as a cured and healthy person. Researchers want tissues from a live body, not from a dead one.

"All our efforts were geared toward bringing him back to Boston on a stretcher alive, not in a coffin.

"That is why both Mr. Spencer and Dr. Parker disappeared, never to return again, as soon as they found out that his death was imminent. I had to come to tell you everything, since I do not know if I will see tomorrow, if I have outlived the need of the foundation, or if I must move on to some other projects for charming people to their death or destruction. Now you see, Doc, I am tied by diamond chains out of which it is impossible for me to get out even if I wanted to. The attraction of *diamond* whips, glittering gold, and the allure of mysterious adventures were too much to pass. My addiction to digging into people's thoughts and deep into their subconscious, breaking into the codes of their secret programs, is too thrilling to me, not to be consumed. My clairvoyant-like predictions shrouded by scientific reasoning frequently enchanted the rich, famous and geniuses, which had led them to their ruin.

"You must think I must be tired and repentant of it all. On the contrary, this is the beginning of a new era. The only one person I respect is the professor, whose intellect and power of realistic imagination frequently amazes me. As I probed more and more into people's mind, the intrigue of their thinking sometimes puzzled me, which would take weeks, months, and years to crack and decode. At times I find, the path is beyond my ability to trade, but rarely did I change course. My professor is an amazing and outstanding thinker, and the forces all around him, I believe, are impregnable. No one can harm him. Not even Mr. Spencer and Dr. Parker. They need him for their survival.

"We are all now tied to each other with diamond chains. Mr. Spencer is well aware of my clear understanding and in-depth knowledge of his plans, programs, and above all his modus operandi. Mr. Spencer's absolute respect and trust in my ability is beyond any doubt—his dependence on me for meticulous and perfect performance for his agenda, without raising any suspicion or causing any waves from authority. He respects my ability to focus on the exact issue and my ability to analyze and synthesize the best results for his use, including blackmailing others. I have kept myself out of this aspect of his operation, and he appears to like it that way. He needed men of international repute, like our professor, as a facade to his operation, totally without the knowledge of these innocent intellectuals.

"Now that James is gone, Mr. Spencer and his men are prowling for another James so that our professor can continue his research, allowing Mr. Spencer and his people to become billionaires.

"What is there for me? The excitement, adventure, and intellectual battleground he provides for me. I do not mind being tied by his diamond chains.

"But something else is missing. I engineered the separation of James's family with lies, pretentions, and misinformation, which I had to do to keep James unwaveringly compliant to our plan and continuing to participate in the plasmapheresis. I felt that the family was likely to be a negative force to achieve our goal. However, I made sure that James's family's life is not threatened; they will not face a life of poverty and distress or become destitute, nor will the children's education falter now that James is gone. That I would have difficulty living with. After all, I am also a woman. I had to protect the family from Spencer's 'pogrom,' at any cost. Which I did."

THE END

About the Author

Kamalendu Malaker has spent the last fifty years working with leading experts in the field of oncology. He trained to become a physician at the University of Calcutta in India and earned his doctorate in cell biology from the University of London. Having trained in oncology in Oxford and the Royal Postgraduate Medical School of London University and received his oncology degree from the Royal College, Malaker became the senior registrar and clinical tutor in radiation oncology at the University of London.

Malaker also served as a research officer at the Dana Farber Cancer Center at Harvard University. Additionally, he published the first cancer journal of India in 1962, is credited with helping establish oncology as a clinical discipline, and has since written hundreds of scientific articles. Malaker is currently a professor of oncology and internal medicine at Ross University and head of oncology at Dominica Princess Margaret Hospital.

Malaker and his wife, Baljit, live in Winnipeg, Canada. They have one adult daughter and a granddaughter.

Made in the USA
Columbia, SC
27 April 2018